'I wanted you hired you!'

'For the campaign, or ...'

'What do you think?'

'I think you planned it this way—I think you chose this place because you ... want to ...'

Ross completed her sentence with a word so explicit it made Alysha choke. 'And what's more, so do you. Don't even try to deny it— your body-language gives you away!'

Dear Reader

Falling in love is exciting...but we all know that it *can* be complicated! For instance, what would you do if the man of your dreams happened to be your father's worst enemy? That's the dilemma faced by Charlotte Lamb's heroine next month in DEADLY RIVALS, the second book in her compelling new series—don't miss it! And you'll find some thrilling love-stories in *this* month's selection, too. We hope you enjoy this one!

The Editor

Susanne McCarthy grew up in South London but she always wanted to live in the country, and shortly after her marriage she moved to Shropshire with her husband. They live in a house on a hill with lots of dogs and cats. She loves to travel—but she loves to come home. As well as her writing, she still enjoys her career as a teacher in adult education, though she only works part-time now.

Recent titles by the same author:

DANGEROUS ENTANGLEMENT
NO PLACE FOR LOVE

PRACTISED DECEIVER

BY

SUSANNE McCARTHY

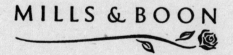

MILLS & BOON

*MILLS & BOON and the Rose Device
are trademarks of the publisher.
Harlequin Mills & Boon Limited,
Eton House, 18-24 Paradise Road, Richmond, Surrey, TW9 1SR
This edition published by arrangement with Harlequin Enterprises B.V.*

© Susanne McCarthy 1995

ISBN 0 263 78983 7

*Set in Times Roman 10.5 on 12 pt
01-9505-56484 C*

Made and printed in Great Britain

CHAPTER ONE

'Don't want it? Whaddya mean, you don't want it?' In moments of extreme stress, Barbara Lange's well-modulated voice had a tendency to slip back into her native Brooklynese. 'Listen, honey, *everybody's* been after that contract. Don't you realise what it means? Not only is it worth a fortune, it's guaranteed to launch your career into orbit! I damn near busted a gut getting you on the short list—you've *gotta* want it!'

'I'm...sorry, Bobbie.' Alysha shifted the telephone into her left hand and held out her right for the stylist to paint her long fingernails with plum-coloured lacquer. 'I had no idea you'd even thought of putting me up for it. Anyway,' she added with a characteristic lack of conceit, 'it probably doesn't matter—I doubt if I'd get it.'

'Are you kidding?' her agent demanded trenchantly. 'Honey, the minute you walked through my door I knew you were gonna be a star! What's got into you? It's not like you to be backward in snapping up a break like this. I'll tell you, there must be a coupla hundred girls out there would give Ross Elliot their right arm to be the Lozier Girl—along with any other part of their anatomy he happened to take a fancy to!' she added with a rich chuckle.

Alysha's soft mouth twisted into a wry smile. She had no doubt whatsoever that there were plenty of girls who would be more than willing to offer Ross

Elliot whatever he wanted—and not just in the hope of furthering their careers. And she had every reason to know that he wouldn't hesitate for a moment to take advantage of their foolishness.

She had only met him once, and that had been five years ago, but that single encounter had been enough; he had succeeded in that one short afternoon in putting her off the whole idea of a modelling career. It was only personal circumstances that had driven her back—but she had been careful to avoid any further contact with him.

So far that hadn't proved difficult. Though he was still known to the public as a top photographer, in the intervening years he had set up his own very successful advertising agency—and it wasn't the sort that used struggling beginners. Maybe she should have known that as her career progressed she was bound to run into him again—but she wasn't sure if she was quite ready for it yet.

'I...do appreciate all you've done, Bobbie,' she responded carefully. Barbara didn't know she'd even met Ross before—no one did; it was a secret she had been too ashamed to tell. 'But... Well, to be honest, it's the thought of working with him that's putting me off. He's...got such a reputation...'

'Do you mean personally, or professionally?' Barbara queried, conceding a hint of sympathy.

'Both!'

The older woman laughed. 'Listen, honey, you can cope with him. Sure, he's a bit of a slave-driver, but you've never had any problems with hard work—you're one of the most reliable girls I've ever had on my books. And as for the rest—if you ask me, a lot of that's just wishful thinking on the part of a lot of very silly girls. They should be so lucky!'

'Alysha? We're ready for you.' The photographer's assistant stuck his head into the trailer.

She acknowledged him with a nod. 'I'm sorry, Bobbie, I have to go now...'

'He's doing us lunch on Wednesday,' Barbara pleaded urgently. 'He's seen your portfolio and the video of that shampoo thing you did, and I guess he wants to give you the final once-over in person. Look, you probably won't have to see too much of him anyway—he spends most of his time behind a desk these days, not behind a camera. Just come along and meet him, talk it over, huh? It's just a go-see—I swear I won't push you into anything you're not happy with.'

Alysha sighed, and then laughed wryly; she couldn't pretend that she was busy on Wednesday—Barbara would already have checked that with the girl who booked all her jobs. It would be a tremendous boost for the agency to get a prestigious contract like this for one of its girls. And she owed Barbara a great deal—she had taken her on as a complete beginner when, at twenty, she was already three or four years older than most girls starting out, giving her the chance of earning the sort of money she needed. Now was her chance to pay some of that back.

'All right,' she conceded, trying not to sound too reluctant. 'Lunch, Wednesday.'

'Good girl,' Barbara chuckled. 'I knew you wouldn't let me down.'

'Alysha...?'

'Coming. See you, Bobbie.'

She put down the phone, careful not to allow herself to frown—it would ruin the perfect *maquillage* that

Sharon, the make-up artist on the shoot, had taken
so long to apply. Rising gracefully to her feet, careful
not to disturb the artless tumble of midnight-dark
curls that fell halfway down her back, she stepped
down from the trailer.

The rich plum-coloured swirl of her silk dress lov-
ingly moulded the slender curves of her figure and
glowed against the flawless honey-gold of her skin.
She owed her almond-shaped eyes, flecked with
amber, to her Malaysian grandmother, but the self-
discipline that enabled her to maintain her poise and
smile through endless tedious hours of being photographed she had developed herself.

Shooting in the middle of Trafalgar Square on a
Monday afternoon, it was inevitable that they had
drawn quite a crowd. Envious office-girls gazed wide-
eyed at the panoply of lights and reflectors and cameras, and the handsome couple in evening clothes
waltzing on the edge of one of Lutyens' fountains,
with the elegant stone facade of the National Gallery
in the background. From the outside, it must seem
like a glamorous dream.

It had seemed like that to her once, she mused wryly
as she moved with practised grace, showing off the
fabulous dress to best advantage. At seventeen, up in
London without the knowledge either of her parents
or of the headmistress of her exclusive Sussex
boarding-school, she had been about as naïve as they
came.

And Ross Elliot had had no scruples whatsoever
about taking advantage of her; he was a rat of the
first water...

*   *   *

The studio was in the heart of London's trendy fashion and theatre district around Covent Garden. It took her a while to find it in the tangle of narrow, old-fashioned streets; she walked past the door twice before she spotted the discreet name-plate: Ross Elliot—Photographic Studio. Ross Elliot had no need to advertise his location ostentatiously.

Drawing in a deep, steadying breath, she rang the bell—and was startled when an abrupt voice close to her ear responded, 'Yup?'

Blinking at the entry-phone in surprise, she managed an unsteady, 'Er...hello. It's...Alysha Fordham-Jones. I've an appointment with Mr Elliot.'

'First floor,' the voice instructed, and the door buzzed and clicked open.

Her heart pounding, she stepped inside, closing the door behind her. She was in a small, narrow hallway, lit up with a row of industrial-design spotlights suspended from the high ceiling; the floor was of bare boards, sanded and gleaming, and the walls were starkly white, hung with several huge framed black-and-white prints of gleaming sports cars, shot close up and from low angles, striking and dramatic.

For a moment she hesitated, a little daunted by the realisation that she was actually here, in Ross Elliot's studio, and about to meet him face to face. Suddenly it was all beginning to seem less of a good idea than it had when she had planned it so carefully, poring eagerly over every magazine article she could find about the glamorous lives of the super-models who jetted around the world from one catwalk to the next, posing for the world's top photographers.

But if anyone could make her dreams come true, release her from the stultifying boredom of her nice,

respectable, middle-class family and the terminal
tedium of school into a world of excitement and ad-
venture, it was Ross Elliot; he was the best, as famous
as any of the models he photographed.

And after all, she had come all this way, taking quite
a chance of getting caught playing hooky from
school—she wasn't going to chicken out now.
Screwing up her courage, she climbed the spiral
staircase that led up to the first floor.

She found herself in a spacious reception area, decorated in the same style as the downstairs hall; a large
window, draped with a casual swag of bleached
muslin, looked out over the lively piazza in front of
Covent Garden itself, with its colourful street per-
formers and Aladdin's cave of exotic little shops and
market stalls.

There was a desk in one corner and as she recognised the man standing beside it an odd little *frisson*
of heat feathered down her spine; everything she had
read about him had warned her that Ross Elliot was
not a man to suffer fools gladly, and that impression
was strongly reinforced as she gazed at him in an awe-
struck daze.

He had to be something over six feet tall, and he
was wearing a faded denim shirt that moulded an impressive breadth of shoulder. His dark hair was drawn
back into a ponytail, and he wore a gold earring in
one ear, but there was nothing effeminate about him—
nothing at all. He was uncompromisingly male, still
branded with the stamp of the tough streets of
Glasgow where he had grown up. And he had a
magnetic physical aura that made her mouth go
suddenly dry.

He didn't even bother to look up as she advanced tentatively into the room; he was bent over the desk, studying a sheet of contact-prints, scribbling over them with a red china-pen, and without lifting his head he called out, 'Tina?'

A pint-sized dynamo in a scarlet T-shirt and leopard-print leggings darted in through a door behind the desk. 'Oh, hi,' she greeted Alysha with a smile as broad as her Australian twang. 'You're the two o'clock, right?' She ran one purple varnished fingertip down the appointment book on the desk. 'Alysha Fordham-Jones. I'm sorry, I don't seem to have taken a note of which agency sent you along?'

'I . . . wasn't sent by an agency,' Alysha confessed apologetically. 'I made the appointment myself.'

'Oh . . .' The other girl hesitated, uncertain. 'Ross?'

He straightened, not troubling to conceal his irritation at having to drag his attention away from what he had been doing, and Alysha found herself subjected to a coolly detached appraisal from a pair of deep-set eyes the colour of hardened steel. 'I only work with girls sent by a reputable agency,' he informed her dismissively.

She felt a rush of pink to her cheeks. 'Oh . . . I'm sorry—I . . . didn't know,' she stammered, disconcerted both by his manner and by something else she couldn't quite define; maybe it was because for at least the past year she had grown accustomed to invoking stunned admiration in most of the callow young men she was allowed to associate with, and to be confronted with six foot four of mature, hard-ground male who seemed completely indifferent to her charms had come as something of a shock.

'Well, now you do,' he responded, turning his attention back to his task.

It was that offhand arrogance that stung her into a countering disdain. 'I can pay,' she informed him in a tone of haughty condescension. She put her hand into her bag, and drew out her purse. 'Cash.'

She had been saving up her allowance for weeks—if she was going to be a model she would have to give up sweets and crisps anyway—and not knowing how much the session would cost she had brought a hundred pounds with her, in crisp ten pound notes she had drawn out of the post office that morning.

Ross Elliot lifted his eyes slowly to look at the money, and then to her face—and the glint of icy anger she saw in them made her insides shiver. Somehow she had insulted him far more than she had intended ... She was just about to apologise when he smiled, a smile that didn't reach those glacial eyes.

'So you want to be a model, Miss Fordham-Jones?' he queried, the voice with its rough-edged Glaswegian accent quiet but unmistakably laced with menace. 'All right.' He held out his hand, and dumbly she put the money into it. He didn't bother to count it, just dropped it into a drawer in the desk in front of him. 'Show her the changing-room, Tina.'

The other girl glanced at him in frank bewilderment, but met only a blank response, so with a small shrug of her shoulders she turned to Alysha. 'This way,' she invited, opening the far door and ushering her through into a long, narrow passage. 'Have you brought some different outfits with you?'

Alysha nodded. 'Er ... yes. A trouser-suit, and an evening dress, and a swimsuit. Is that all right?'

'Fine. We'll start with the trouser-suit. And I'll give you a hand with your make-up and hair—usually the agency would fix up a team to work on the shoot, but...'

'But I wasn't sent by an agency,' Alysha concluded with a wry smile. 'I'm really sorry about that—I hope...I mean, I wouldn't want you to get into trouble over it or anything.'

Tina laughed. 'Oh, no—don't worry about it,' she assured her blithely. 'Look, you don't want to let Ross scare you, you know—he's all right really, once you get to know him. His bark's a lot worse than his bite.'

Alysha cautiously decided to reserve judgement on that one.

Tina opened a door at the end of the passage, and flicked a light switch. Alysha found herself in a small, brightly lit changing-room. There was a white-painted dressing-table, surmounted by a huge mirror with light bulbs all round it, and another long mirror on the wall. On a hatstand in the corner was an eclectic collection of hats and scarves and belts and bead necklaces, and on a shelf above the small hand-basin were rows of half-empty bottles of nail varnish, cans of hairspray, and every shade of lipstick the creative imagination of the cosmetic houses of Europe and America could dream up.

'Here we are,' Tina announced. 'I'll leave you to get changed, and then I'll come back in ten minutes and we can start on your face. Oh, and I'll bring the model-release for you to sign. Ross always insists on it—it's just so he can use the pictures if he wants to.'

Alysha couldn't imagine that he would, but she nodded. 'Oh... Yes. Thank you very much.'

She put down her bag, and sank down on the stool in front of the dressing-table, gazing around her in a kind of awe. Just think of all the fabulous top models who must have sat here before her...! Would she be one of them one day—her services in demand from all the top designers for their catwalk shows, her face on the covers of her favourite glossy magazines?

At this moment, to be honest, she would really much rather have run away, jumped on the train back to school. But she wasn't going to let Ross Elliot intimidate her. And after all, he had taken her hundred pounds—and she didn't much fancy the idea of asking him to give it back.

But half an hour later all her reservations were forgotten. She had thought she was quite good at putting on make-up, but the effect Tina had achieved was stunning. With subtle skill she had highlighted her delicate cheekbones, emphasising the soft curve of her mouth and lending a strange, smokey mystery to her eyes. Then she had twisted her hair up into a simple, elegant style that made her look a good five years older.

'There—you look great!' Tina approved with satisfaction. 'Don't you think so?'

Alysha stared back at her own reflection in that enormous mirror, bemused by the transformation. 'Y...yes,' she murmured. 'Thank you very much.'

'I'll tell Ross you're ready,' Tina added, her eyes dancing. 'He'll be absolutely knocked out when he sees you!'

Alysha doubted that—he had studied too many really beautiful women through the eye of his camera to be even remotely impressed by her. But even so, that unfamiliar person she could see, gazing back at her with her own amber-flecked eyes, looked very much the part.

Her mouth felt a little dry as she walked through into the studio. Ross was already there, setting up the lighting around a simple set that consisted of a tall wooden three-legged stool in front of a backdrop of bleached cotton draped from a track hanging from the ceiling. He didn't even glance up as she came in, just waved her into place with a casual gesture of his hand.

She wasn't sure what to do, so she perched on the stool, one foot on the floor, her hands clenched in her lap.

Ross bent to look through his camera. 'Try to look a little less as if you're about to have a tooth extracted,' he appealed, a sardonic inflection in his voice.

Behind him, Tina placed her hands on her hips, turning her shoulders slightly. With a grateful smile, Alysha mirrored her actions.

'Better,' Ross approved, oblivious of his assistant's prompting. 'Lift your chin. Slide that left leg forward a little more.' He moved to adjust one of the lights a little. 'Tina, if you've nothing better to do than stand there, go and turn the tape-deck on.'

Tina grinned wryly, and obeyed, filling the room with the sounds of Genesis, and then with a small wave to Alysha she slipped out of the room.

The next couple of hours were the hardest work Alysha had ever known—if she had dreamed of modelling as a glamorous career, she was quickly finding out that standing perfectly still for endless moments, or repeating the same small movement over and over until he was completely satisfied, made her ache with cramp until she longed to scream.

As the afternoon wore on, she became convinced that he had only agreed to do the session to teach her some kind of lesson. He was ruthless in his demands, barking instructions and impatiently critical when she was wooden or awkward. But though she was exhausted and close to tears, she refused to let him defeat her.

The sensational backless black evening dress she had splurged so much money on drew no comment from him whatsoever; Tina had changed her make-up, using a darker shade of lipstick and more shadow on her eyes, creating an image of sensual sophistication, but she might as well have been wearing a paper bag over her head.

It was getting late by the time they were ready to start on the swimsuit shots, and Ross had sent Tina out to pick up something from the dry-cleaners. She seemed to work like a galley-slave for him, without expecting even a word of thanks, Alysha reflected as she brushed out her hair to let it fall loose around her shoulders; she was probably in love with him.

She was a little nervous of posing in front of him wearing only the cerise-pink designer swimsuit she hadn't dared let anyone else see; cut high on the thigh and low between her small, firm breasts, it clung like a second skin. But Ross Elliot betrayed not the slightest sign that he found her blossoming curves even remotely alluring; his indifference was humiliating—she wasn't used to being treated in such an off-hand manner. Everyone else thought she was beautiful, they were always saying she ought to be a model—but apparently he didn't agree. And he ought to know—he was the professional. Had all this been for nothing, after all?

They had been working for twenty minutes when he told her to take a break while he loaded his cameras with fresh film. With a sigh of relief, Alysha stepped down from the set, glad to be able to stretch her weary limbs a little. During breaks in the shooting she had wandered around the studio, gazing enviously at the pictures taped all over the walls; many of the models she recognised—beautiful women, the ones whose faces regularly graced the covers of *Vogue* and *Harper's*. One day...?

There was a low table and some chairs at the back of the studio, for meetings, and on the table was a thick bound folder of mounted photographs. She flipped it casually open to look; the pictures were all of those same top models—and they had posed for him in various states of elegant undress, some of them even naked! Yet there was nothing at all pornographic about them; they were pure art—strong images of women confident in their own sexuality, photographed by a man who had a genuine liking and respect for them . . .

'Do you like them?'

She stared as Ross spoke close behind her—in his battered old tennis-shoes he had made no sound across the studio floor. 'Oh...yes,' she stammered, her heart thudding so loudly she was afraid he would hear it. 'They're . . . fabulous.'

A strange glint was lurking in the depths of those mesmerising grey eyes. 'How would you like to try some like that?' he asked, nodding towards them.

Her cheeks flamed scarlet; the thought had already crossed her mind—maybe that would be the way to get some positive reaction out of him! But she had told herself at once not to be so stupid; she could never compete with the stunning creatures in those pictures. And besides, the thought of taking her clothes off in front of Ross Elliot . . .

'Oh . . . No, I couldn't,' she protested breathlessly. 'I . . .'

She felt the chill of his anger, tautly controlled. 'Suit yourself,' he responded with a dismissive shrug of his wide shoulders. 'If you don't want to do it, that's fine by me—there's no need to come on like some prudish little schoolgirl. Do I look like one of the dirty-mac brigade, for Pete's sake?'

She swallowed hard, shaking her head. 'I'm sorry. I didn't mean . . .'

He seemed to relent a little, conceding a grim smile. 'Look,' he coaxed, his voice taking on a gentler note as he flipped over the pages of the folder. 'Look at those women. You know who they are. Do you think they'd have let me take those pictures if they hadn't trusted me? I don't have any ulterior motive—if I want a woman, I don't have to resort to underhand tricks, believe me. I want to take your picture because you're beautiful—that's all there is to it.'

She gazed up at him, caught in the spell of those strangely changeable silver-grey eyes. Did he *really* think she was beautiful? Suddenly she knew that that was the only thing in the world that mattered. His brusque treatment of her was forgotten—she wanted only to please him . . .

'A . . . all right,' she whispered shyly. 'I'll do it.'

He smiled slowly; not in triumphant gloating, but simply in straightforward acknowledgement of her agreement. 'There's a batik thing in the changing-room,' he said. 'Sling it around your hips, and then come back in here—we'll start like that.'

She nodded, her mouth dry. Of course it would be all right, she told herself reassuringly; this was no seedy back-street operation—Ross Elliot was one of the most respected names in the business. And as he had so caustically pointed out, if he wanted someone to... sleep with, there would be plenty of willing candidates, she was quite sure of that. It would really be rather conceited of her to think he was plotting to... seduce her. But even so, the thought of standing there in front of him, half-naked...

The batik was a large square of cotton, printed in vivid shades of red, orange, yellow and green. She unfolded it and shook it out, and then, setting her jaw in determination, she slipped out of her swimsuit and wrapped the batik around her hips—there was quite enough fabric to wear it like a sarong, but her hands were shaking so much it was difficult to tie the knot.

'Ready?' he called, a touch of that now-familiar impatience returning to his voice—she actually found that quite reassuring.

'Y... yes. Coming.'

Hugging her arms protectively across her naked breasts, she stepped out into the studio. The lights felt hot on her skin, and her knees were trembling so much that she had to perch on the wooden stool or she was afraid she would fall. Ross was adjusting a lens, and he glanced up, a flicker of irritation crossing that hard-boned, handsome face.

'It's not going to be any good like that,' he pointed out drily. 'Put your arms down.'

Hesitantly, she obeyed. Her breasts were small and firm, the tender nipples like dainty rosebuds; but now, as she drew in a ragged breath, they seemed to ache and swell beneath his gaze, erotically seductive, wantonly inviting. She saw a small, tense movement in his hard jaw, and realised with a shiver of nervous apprehension that he wasn't quite so professionally detached as he had been pretending to be.

She could feel a hot blush rise to her cheeks; but she had agreed to do this, and he would think she was nothing but a silly little idiot if she refused to go through with it now. Her blood was racing so fast that she felt a little dizzy, so she put her hands behind her to grip the back of the stool, unconsciously arching her back to curve her body provocatively towards him.

'That's good—hold that.' She heard the click and whirr of his camera. 'Now, lift one hand and toss your hair back over your shoulder. Look into the camera—that's it, but don't smile.'

Her body moved to his commands, almost without the conscious involvement of her mind. It was as if his will had taken her over, and he could do whatever he liked with her. Her soft lips were slightly parted, her silken skin glowing and warm; soon he would ask her to take off the sarong and pose completely naked—and she would do it. In the intimacy of the empty studio, all her inhibitions were evaporating in a sweet, melting tide of feminine submissiveness ...

'Damn!' He cursed sharply, and straightened from behind the camera. 'The heat of the lights is making your nipples go soft—they're no good like that in the pictures. We'll have to do something about it.'

She gazed at him, wide-eyed and bewildered, as he walked over to a small refrigerator in the corner, and came back with an ice-cube in his hand.

'Just a small trick of the trade,' he explained, a lilt of teasing in his voice.

She gasped in shock as he ran the ice-cube over her breasts; the delicate peaks responded instantly, puckering into taut buds.

He laughed softly, mockingly. 'So sweet and demure,' he murmured. 'I bet butter wouldn't melt in your mouth—or even an ice-cube!'

Before she had realised what he was going to do, he had popped it between her parted lips—and the next thing she knew he had gathered her up in his arms, and his mouth had closed over hers, warm and persuasive, his tongue swirling sensuously around to hook the melting ice-cube into his own mouth and then slide it back into hers.

She didn't even think of resisting him. She had never known anything like this—it was as if all her dreams had spun together into one magical moment of paradise. Her naked breasts were crushed against the hard wall of his chest, his rough denim shirt rasping deliciously over her sensitised nipples, and she felt as if she was going up in flames...

Quite what would have happened if they hadn't been interrupted Alysha had never cared to speculate; it had been fortunate that that sensation of going up in flames had been no illusion—one of the lights had tipped over against a paper screen, setting it smouldering.

By the time Ross had dealt with it, she had come to her senses and fled back to the changing-room, dressing at top speed and stuffing her things into her bag, escaping from the studio before he could come looking for her. She had changed her mind—she didn't want to be a model after all.

She had never told anyone what had happened that afternoon. She had hurried back to school, fortunate that the excuse she had used to cover her absence hadn't been detected, and had buried herself in her studies—to such good effect that she had achieved excellent grades in her A-levels, and been accepted by one of the top universities to study to be a veterinary surgeon.

And that would have been that; but, just as she was about to take her second year exams, the privileged life she had always known had come to an abrupt end. Her father had been implicated in a massive share fraud and, rather than face the humiliation of a public trial, he had committed suicide—leaving his family to cope unprepared with the chill frost of poverty.

With her mother still in a state of shock, Alysha had telephoned her father's eldest brother for help—only to have it very forcibly brought home to her how deeply the family had disapproved of old Colonel Fordham-Jones's scandalous second marriage, and their absolute refusal to have anything to do with the outcome of that unwelcome liaison. And she had known she could expect little more from her mother's family—they were of the old school, stiff-upper-lip, stand-on-your-own-two feet persuasion. After having had one uncle put down the phone on her, she'd be damned if she'd go crawling to any other relatives. They'd manage without anyone else—somehow she'd find a way to cope.

And so at the age of nineteen, it had fallen on her slim shoulders to try to earn enough money to keep a roof over their heads and pay her younger brother's school fees. Forced to give up on her own ambitions, she had left university, and traded on the only asset she had left—her looks.

This time she had known better—she had gone to a proper model agency. And she had been lucky—Barbara Lange had been impressed with the holiday snaps she had taken along, and had arranged test shots for her. And although even at the ripe old age of twenty she had been viewed as something of a late starter in the business she had made rapid progress, through the hard slog of catalogue work to the giddy heights of the catwalks and glossies she had once coveted so desperately.

And now with what seemed like an almost inevitable working of fate, her path was to cross Ross Elliot's once again. Why had he put her name on the short list? Did he think that now she was older, and—he would assume—more experienced, she would be more amenable to his practised seduction routine? That she wouldn't run away in a panic this time?

Well, if that was the case, he would soon find out his mistake, she mused grimly. Oh, she wouldn't panic or run away—she had learned a number of much more effective ways of dealing with unwanted advances. He would be in for quite an unwelcome surprise.

CHAPTER TWO

THE taxi drew to a halt outside the smart restaurant, and Alysha climbed out. She was greeted by a chorus of wolf-whistles from a building site across the street, and a middle-aged man in a grey suit, staring back at her over his shoulder as he passed, bumped into a lamp-post. Suppressing a small smile of amusement, she stepped into the restaurant.

She had dressed with great care for this luncheon date, in a suit of ivory linen-silk, cut with a stunning simplicity of line that skimmed over her slender curves. Her trademark hair was caught well back from her face to highlight her delicate bone-structure, and rippled in a dark glossy mane down her back, and the tall heels of her tan shoes took her to a willowy six feet one.

They were the highest heels she could find—but she would still have to look up to meet Rose Elliot's eyes, she reminded herself with a taut little *frisson* of apprehension. She had done her best to talk herself into readiness for this meeting, but her heart was still beating much too fast, making her feel a little light-headed.

The restaurant was busy, but she saw him right away; he was on the far side of the room, and as he glanced up those compelling steel-grey eyes locked on hers from the far side of the room, like a laser-gun locking on its target. He was watching her, waiting for her to come to him; and for one uncomfortable moment the memories of the last time they had met swirled in her brain, and she felt as if she were again wearing only that low-slung sarong, her breasts flushed and naked, her delicate pink nipples pertly inviting his insolent survey...

'Good afternoon, Miss Jones. May I show you to your table?'

With an effort of will she pulled herself together, nodding a pleasant acknowledgement to the head waiter, and, holding herself gracefully erect, she followed him between the well-spaced tables, long practice enabling her to seem unaware of the lascivious or envious stares that pursued her.

Ross rose to his feet, holding out his hand to greet her with a polite formality that threw her slightly off balance; he seemed to be behaving as if they had never met before.

'Miss Fordham-Jones—thank you for joining us.'

'Good...afternoon, Mr Elliot,' she managed to respond, placing her hand in his for the briefest moment and withdrawing it before there was any risk of him noticing the slight tremor of nervousness that she couldn't quite control. Bobbie was already seated at the table, halfway through a white wine spritzer, and Alysha greeted her with a smile that concealed her relief at not finding herself alone with Ross. 'Hello, Bobbie. I hope I'm not late?'

'Of course not—we were early,' Bobbie assured her warmly. 'Have a seat.'

The head waiter was holding out a chair for her, and one of his minions was hovering with the menu; she accepted both with a brief word of thanks, making a swift selection of Charentais melon, followed by seabass in a lime and lemon sauce which sounded delicious.

On the far side of the table, Ross was engaged in conversation with Bobbie, which gave her an opportunity to study him covertly. He hadn't changed much in five years, she mused: the earring had gone, and so had the ponytail—his hair was now neatly trimmed, just a few wayward strands falling over his forehead. But he still wore the same casual denims, making no concession to the elegance of the restaurant, and beneath them his body was as hard-muscled and powerful as ever.

And there was still the same arrogance in that rough-hewn face, with its angular cheekbones and uncompromising jaw, still the same hint of cruelty around that hard mouth. And he still possessed a potent physical magnetism that was very difficult to ignore.

But though he had the look of a street-fighter, there had to be a lot more to him than that, she reflected thoughtfully. The world of fashion photography was highly competitive, and it must have taken more than just a good eye for a picture, and a smooth line of chat with the models, for him to have clawed his way to the top of it.

And even that had only been a means to an end for him, it seemed. It had created something of a stir when he had set up his own advertising agency—it was quite an unusual move for a photographer, to take on the business side of the industry. But he had been very successful; with his reputation, all the top freelance talent in London had been queueing up to work for him, and *Élan* had quickly become one of the most prestigious hot-shops in town, putting together some of the most strikingly creative campaigns of the past few years.

Perhaps it wasn't surprising, after all, that he should have forgotten their first meeting. She must have been one of dozens—hundreds—of naïve young hopefuls who had passed through his studio. And he probably tried the same underhand trick on all of them.

And yet . . . Was it just her imagination, or had she detected a faint trace of irony in his greeting? And why had he used the double-barrelled part of her surname so deliberately? She never used it professionally, preferring the simpler, snappier Alysha Jones. *Did* he remember . . . ?

'I've been telling Bobbie the details of the campaign,' he informed her; he was lounging back in his seat, regarding Alysha across the table with that coolly disinterested appraisal she remembered so vividly from their first meeting. And, to her chagrin, she found that it still had the power to discomfit her.

'It sounds terrific!' Bobbie put in, her eyes alight with enthusiasm. 'A real winner.'

'The key concept is danger,' he went on. She had almost forgotten that voice—slightly husky, as if his vocal cords had been sandpapered by the raw Clydeside air of his youth. 'We're going to be emphasising the danger to the skin from excessive exposure to the sun. The lab people at Loziers have come up with a new UBA/UBV sunblock which is being introduced across the whole product range.'

'And the ingredients are all from natural sources, of course,' Bobbie assured her. 'There's been no animal testing. Alysha feels very strongly about that,' she added to Ross. 'She's frequently turned down even very well-paid jobs because she won't wear fur or use cosmetics that involved cruelty to animals.'

Those steel-grey eyes glinted with unmistakable cynicism. 'She's lucky she can afford to stand by her principles,' he remarked, a sardonic inflection in his voice.

Alysha returned him a frosty glare. Did he think it was no more than a fashionable stance, taken by someone who would barely notice the sacrifice? Well, she certainly wasn't going to disabuse him; her money struggles were a secret she guarded behind a carefully constructed illusion spun of rich-girl gloss and expensive designer clothes—bought wholesale or second-hand.

Very few people knew of the scandal about her father—fortunately it had attracted little publicity outside the financial circles of the City. And that was exactly the way she wanted it; the shame of finding out what he had done had been extremely painful, and she still hadn't really got over it.

'Could we stick to discussing the campaign?' she requested, her voice laced with icy dignity.

A faintly mocking smile flickered at the corners of that hard mouth, but he acceded smoothly to her request. 'There'll be massive coverage in the glossies, as well as television slots and personal appearances. The Lozier Girl embodies the image of Lozier—a hedonistic indulgence for the woman who can afford that little bit more. That's why we insist on an exclusive contract; any other work you do has to be subject to my personal approval—we don't want the Lozier Girl showing up in some shoddy mail-order catalogue. And of course we'll be paying very handsomely for the privilege,' he added on a note of dry sarcasm.

Instinctively she was on the defensive, watchful for any hint that he had seen through her façade. 'Money isn't my primary consideration,' she informed him with lofty disdain. 'I'm interested solely in furthering my career.'

A glint of amusement lit those steel-grey eyes. 'I stand corrected.'

She acknowledged the apology with a slight inclination of her head. 'You ... said there would be personal appearances?' she enquired a little stiffly.

He leaned back in his seat, taking a sip of the Perrier water he was drinking—he was reputed never to touch alcohol. 'It's going to be a global campaign, involving a great deal of travel. There'll be promotional visits to major cities throughout Europe and North America, Japan, Australia—I hope you have plenty of stamina?'

Alysha mirrored his coolly sardonic manner, lifting one finely arched eyebrow a fraction of an inch. 'I can cope,' she returned levelly.

'I'm glad to hear it. It would be a major inconvenience if you were to become ill.'

'I'm never ill, Mr Elliot,' she assured him, her eyes glittering. 'I've never missed a single appointment, or even been late, as Barbara will confirm.'

'You certainly have an excellent professional reputation,' he accorded, a sardonic inflection in his voice. 'Otherwise I wouldn't even have considered you.'

Why *had* he considered her? she wondered with a lingering sense of disquiet. She was under no illusions—there were dozens of other girls with similar attributes to herself, who could meet the exacting criteria he had laid down. But the gossip-machine, normally so efficient, hadn't come up with a single other name that was in line for this contract.

Why her?

'What's the timetable for the campaign?' she asked, her voice commendably even.

'Phase one will be the television commercials, co-ordinated with saturation coverage in all the major fashion monthlies,' he explained succinctly. 'The main launch will be at the beginning of April, and we'll be pushing heavily right through into August/September. We'll be shooting the video for the commercials simultaneously with the stills, mostly on location in Thailand.'

'Starting when?'

'December.' He lifted one dark eyebrow in sardonic enquiry as a flicker of uncertainty passed across her face. 'Is that a problem?'

'Only if it would mean being away over Christmas,' she responded in carefully measured tones. 'I usually spend it with my family.' And she could just imagine her mother's reaction if she were to announce that she would be away for the festive season!

He shrugged his wide shoulders in a gesture of almost contemptuous dismissal. 'We have to fit in with the climate out there—December is the time when it's most likely to be dry and comparatively cool,' he returned brusquely. 'Whether you'll be home in time for Christmas depends on the shooting schedule and how well the work goes.'

'I see.' She wasn't going to waste her breath arguing with him; she really wouldn't put it past him to cancel Christmas—he was just the sort of task-driven, ambitious rat who would, and be damned to anyone else's feelings.

'Alysha's diary can be clear by then,' Bobbie assured him, crisply efficient. 'There are a few things lined up, but we can reassign them easily enough—it won't be a problem.' She turned to Alysha, her eyes sparkling. 'I *do* envy you going to Thailand—it has to be one of my all-time favourite places. I hope you'll give her a chance to do a little sightseeing, Ross,' she added, slanting him a teasing glance. 'You really must see the Grand Temple in Bangkok—it's just fascinating.'

Alysha forced herself to look Ross straight in the eye, unflinching. 'Mr Elliot hasn't confirmed yet whether or not he's going to offer me the contract,' she pointed out coolly.

Again she found herself subjected to that detached professional assessment, and she struggled to return him a level gaze. Though she had long grown out of the adolescent vanity that had been so affronted by his indifference at their first meeting, recognising that her looks were no more than a fortunate pattern of genetic inheritance that she could exploit to earn her living, she had found that even in the glamorous world of the fashion business, where beauty was the common currency, they gave her an edge, a measure of power, in most situations.

But to Ross Elliot, it seemed, she was no more than a piece of equipment, on a par with the props and the lighting and probably rather less important than the cameras. If he could have replaced her with a china doll, that would do his bidding and never get tired or need a break, he would happily do so.

'Don't cut the hair,' he ordered.

Her eyes flashed in icy indignation; she had never had any intention of cutting her hair but for one brief moment she found herself toying with the idea, just to defy him. But that would be foolish, she reminded herself briskly—she was a professional, and she was being hired to do a job of work. Her personal feelings mustn't be allowed to come into it.

'Do I take it that that's a yes?' she enquired.

'Do you want it?'

He was forcing her to spar with him, and she felt an odd little tug of visceral excitement in the pit of her stomach. She *did* want it. It was more than just the money—though heaven knew how much she needed that! But having been forced to sacrifice her own aspirations to the need to support her family, she had transferred all her ambition into her modelling career. She wanted to get to the top—and this was a big step in the right direction. And she'd be damned if she'd let Ross Elliot and his mocking grey eyes scare her off!

'Yes, I want it,' she returned, will-power alone keeping her voice steady.

'Then I shall discuss the details with Bobbie.'

For a moment Alysha felt giddy, caught up in a wild vortex of conflicting emotions. Satisfaction, of course, at beating the field to such a lucrative and prestigious contract, and relief that it would absolve her of the ever-present worry about money for at least the foreseeable future; but panic, also, that it would mean seeing far more of this disturbing man than she liked.

Fortunately at that moment the waiter arrived with their starter, and she was able to divert her attention to the cool, delicious melon. She was fortunate that keeping her figure had never been a problem for her; she naturally preferred fresh fruit and vegetables to sweets and pastries, she swam almost every day, and practised the ballet exercises she had enjoyed since childhood, which kept her body strong and supple, able to hold an awkward pose for as long as necessary, or repeat a single movement over and over until the photographer caught the exact fall of limbs and hair that he wanted.

Bobbie glanced across the table at her plate, and sighed enviously. 'Melon! I wish I'd thought of that— I've never been able to get out of the habit of eating rabbit-food.' She forked her green salad around her plate in disgust. 'You girls don't know how lucky you are these days—you're allowed to carry those few extra pounds. When I was in the business, you had to stay as thin as a stick-insect. I'm sure the look's much more attractive now—don't you agree, Ross?'

A flicker of dark amusement danced behind those changeable grey eyes. 'Speaking as a photographer, lean looks good through the camera,' he acknowledged. 'But as a man...I prefer a little more to get hold of.' That disturbingly sensuous mouth curved into a slow smile as he glanced across the table at Alysha. 'Of course, the girl who has good bone-structure *and* nice, well-shaped breasts has a distinct advantage,' he added, the husky timbre of his voice making her shiver. 'Not too large—about the size of a ripe peach is just about right.'

Alysha swallowed thickly, struggling to control the rapid acceleration of her heartbeat. It took a considerable effort of will to stop herself glancing down to check that she really was properly dressed; the way he was looking at her stirred memories so vivid that it seemed as though the years had evaporated, and she was once again the naïve and vulnerable little fool, posing for him half-naked, her breasts aching and ripe beneath his assessing gaze ...

The most sensible course of action, she warned herself astringently, would be to tell him she wasn't interested in the contract, simply to get up right now and walk out; but that would only let him know how deeply she had been affected by what had happened—how deeply she was still affected.

Did he remember? Was this some kind of twisted power-game he was playing for his own amusement? Or did he just not think it worth mentioning? After all, it had meant nothing to him—no doubt he would expect it to mean no more to her.

Well, fine, she could play it like that; her whole career was based on her ability to create illusions—a few deft touches of make-up, a different hairstyle, a change of clothes, and she could be a winsome ingénue one moment, a cool sophisticate the next, a purring sex-kitten or mysteriously exotic, Latin or oriental or suntanned English gamine. That was her stock-in-trade.

'Who else is going to be on the team?' she asked, adopting a pointedly businesslike tone.

'It isn't all tied up yet,' he responded, accepting her change of subject with just the faintest glint of knowing amusement in those cool eyes. 'Alastair Grant will be the make-up man, and Gemma Caldwell the stylist.'

'Gemma?' Bobbie queried, slanting him a look of teasing amusement.

He nodded, seemingly unaware of any reason why employing one of his previous girlfriends should be any cause for surprise. 'She's one of the best in the business.'

'Oh, I agree,' Bobbie conceded graciously. 'And Alastair is an absolute genius, of course. And what about the photographer? Or will you be doing the pictures yourself?'

To Alysha's intense relief he shook his head. 'I'm talking to Harry Keaton.'

Bobbie lifted an enquiring eyebrow. 'Harry? Is he off the sauce?'

'He hasn't had a drink in months,' Ross assured her. 'He's done quite a bit of work for me recently, and he's back to his old form.'

'It's very generous of you to give him the chance,' Bobbie insisted, her eyes glowing.

Ross shrugged his wide shoulders in a gesture of casual dismissal. 'He's an old friend—he helped me a lot in my early days.'

Alysha was barely paying attention to the conversation; she had registered only that Ross wouldn't be taking the pictures himself. But of course he wouldn't—he was the head of a very busy advertising agency now. Even the Lozier contract would be only one of a number of interests. She would probably hardly even see him. What she was feeling could only be relief.

She sipped her wine, struggling to relax the tension in her taut-strung nerve-fibres. On the other side of the table, Ross and Bobbie were laughing together at some piece of wicked gossip that was going the rounds. Watching them covertly from beneath her lashes, Alysha remembered that the two of them had once been an 'item'. It had been quite serious, too, at the time—or so the gossip claimed.

He seemed to have a talent for retaining the friendship of his exes, she mused thoughtfully—although the way Bobbie was flirting with him suggested that she had rather more than mere friendship on her mind! And he didn't seem entirely indifferent, Alysha noted with a stab of something she didn't care to examine too closely; there was a glint of appreciative amusement in his eyes as he responded to that sharp New York wit.

Of course, Barbara Lange was still strikingly beautiful; she had been one of the top models in the business in her day, and though she was now in her late thirties her figure was still as slender as a reed in her chic designer suit, her glossy ash-blonde hair cut in a fashionable bob. Twice divorced, she exuded an air of sophisticated independence: the kind of woman who had no need of a man to lean on. But apparently even she wasn't immune to Ross Elliot's high-octane brand of male sexuality.

Would the two of them get back together? And if they did, why should she care? It meant nothing to her—her own relationship with him would be strictly business; she had seen too many complications for other girls through getting involved with men on location shoots, and she preferred to keep her private life, such as it was, strictly separate. And even if she didn't, the last man she would want to get involved with was Ross Elliot!

They had finished their meal, and the waiter had brought coffee, when Bobbie spotted an acquaintance on the other side of the restaurant, and excused herself to go table-hopping. Left alone with Ross, Alysha absently picked up a coffee spoon and began fiddling with it; it was very difficult to maintain her cool façade when he was sitting there across the table, those smokey grey eyes watching her...

'Have you finished stirring your coffee?' he queried, an inflection of mocking humour in his voice. 'Only I feel I should point out that you haven't put any sugar in it.'

She felt a rush of pink colour her cheeks, and put the spoon down quickly. Damn the man—somehow she just couldn't seem to keep him from getting under her skin! Forcing herself to return him a level look, she enquired, 'When will you be announcing that you've chosen the Lozier Girl?'

'As soon as the contract is signed.'

Her eyes met his with a hint of challenge. 'Who else was on the short list?'

A faint smile curved that intriguing mouth—how was it that it could appear both sensual and cruel at the same time? 'I don't think you really expect me to tell you that,' he countered, fencing with her again. 'It would hardly be...professional.'

'I shall find out,' she reminded him coolly. 'The grapevine is usually pretty efficient.'

He laughed softly. 'Really? Then I'm surprised you bothered to ask me.'

She regarded him with narrowed suspicion. 'How many were on the short list?'

Those steel-grey eyes were glinting with amused appreciation of her perspicacity. 'There wasn't a short list,' he acknowledged. 'I don't work like that. I had a list of prerequisites, and I used my contacts in the business to identify a girl who matched that list. This is a long-term commitment on both sides—to choose someone on the basis of a brief go-see would be like choosing a wife on the basis of a one-night stand.'

Alysha was suddenly conscious of the dryness of her mouth, and lifted her coffee-cup, taking a convulsive swallow that burned her tongue and made her choke. Ross quickly took her cup from her, setting it down as she struggled to regain her breath, all too acutely aware of her scarlet face and the eyes of everyone in the restaurant turned to their table.

'I'm . . . sorry,' she managed, her voice disastrously unsteady. 'It was . . . hotter than I expected.'

'Of course,' he conceded, though the glint of sardonic humour in his eyes warned her that he knew exactly what it was that had disconcerted her.

She could only hope that his other business commitments would prevent him from becoming too closely involved in the Lozier campaign. Their one brief meeting had had a devastating effect on the course of her life; of course she should be much wiser now, five years on—but she had an uncomfortable feeling that maturity and wisdom would prove no defence against that treacherous charm if he chose to deploy it against her again.

'Tennis? What on earth do you want to take up tennis for?' Alysha queried, trying hard to keep the exasperation she was feeling out of her voice.

'I've always enjoyed tennis,' her mother responded peevishly. 'Even though I haven't had much chance to play since I was at school. Besides, it's very good exercise.'

'I'm sure it is,' Alysha acknowledged wryly. 'But did you have to join such an expensive private club?'

'You surely wouldn't expect me to go to the *council* courts?' Audrey Fordham-Jones protested in haughty indignation. 'Anyway, if you want the best coaching you have to go to a good club—it's not the sort of thing you can cut corners on.'

'Yes, but, Mummie, twenty-five pounds for half an hour's couching...? Who have you got?'

'It gets me out of the house,' Audrey countered, sliding into a familiar refrain. 'It's no fun for me, you know, sitting around with nothing to do and no one to talk to. It's all right for you, down there in London, having a good time...'

'Mummie, I have to be in London. If I wasn't working, you wouldn't be able to go to your tennis club at all.'

'I hardly call *that* working,' Audrey responded dismissively. 'Just having your picture taken. If you ask me... Ah, there's Oliver!' she exclaimed, instantly alert to the sound of a car turning on to the drive. 'Dear boy—he promised to try to come home for the weekend, and he always keeps his promises.'

Alysha smiled wryly to herself as her mother jumped to her feet and bustled out into the hall to welcome her younger brother. Oliver had always been the apple of Audrey's eye—he could do no wrong. Considering how spoilt he had been as a child, it was really quite remarkable that he had grown up into such a very pleasant, good-natured young man.

He came into the hall, grinning as usual, his slightly wayward dark hair flopping about his ears, and accepted his mother's hug with tolerant amusement. 'Hi, Mums—hi, Sis. I've brought Nige home for the weekend—is that OK?' He waved a vague hand in the general direction of a lanky, fair-haired young man who had followed him up the steps, and was now hovering bashfully behind him.

Mrs Fordham-Jones frowned at this casual introduction. 'Oh, dear—I wish you'd warned me you were planning to bring a guest,' she protested. 'I would have asked Mrs Potter to get the spare room ready.'

'Oh, there's no need to fuss,' Oliver declared dismissively. 'Nige can sleep on the floor in my room— he's brought a sleeping-bag along.'

'I hope it isn't inconvenient, Mrs Fordham-Jones?' the lad put in diffidently. 'I told Ollie we should have rung first.'

'Not at all,' Audrey insisted, stepping adroitly into her practised role of social hostess. 'Do come in, Nigel. Would you like a cup of tea? I'm sure you must be freezing, driving all the way from London in that dreadful old car of Oliver's. I can't think why he insists on keeping it, instead of getting a new one, but then I suppose those old bangers are all the thing with you young people nowadays, aren't they?'

Oliver exchanged a brief glance of sardonic humour with Alysha. They both knew why he kept the ancient Morris Minor he had bought for a song—because a student grant wouldn't run to the money for a new one, and he was reluctant to accept any more handouts than he had to from his sister.

'Alysha, *do* be a dear and put the kettle on,' Mrs Fordham-Jones requested sweetly. 'I'm afraid it's my housekeeper's day off today,' she added to Nigel, leading the way through to the drawing-room, 'so we're having to muddle through by ourselves. But I think there's still some of Cook's cherry-cake, if you'd like to try it? I don't care what people say, you really can't beat home-made.'

The poor young man had stood transfixed by Alysha from the moment he had stepped through the door, and now he was blushing a deep shade of scarlet at the thought of this goddess being despatched to make him a cup of tea. She took pity on him, smiling with friendly warmth.

'Good afternoon, Nigel,' she greeted him. 'Why don't you go and sit down, and I'll bring the tea through in a minute?'

'Oh... Yes... Thank you...' he choked out inarticulately. 'I... Thank you.'

Alysha slipped off to the kitchen, where a moment later her brother joined her. 'How's it going, then?' he enquired, giving her shoulders an affectionate squeeze. 'Sorry we were late—the old jalopy started over-heating on the A40, and we had to keep stopping and letting her cool down. Has she been driving you batty?' He nodded his head in the general direction of the sitting-room.

She laughed softly, shaking her head. 'No more than usual. She can't help it—it's been very difficult for her these past few years.'

Ollie snorted in derision. 'All that housekeeper and cook stuff—you'd think she'd realise she doesn't fool anyone for a minute. Is that the "home-made" cake?' he added teasingly as Alysha peeled off the shop-wrapper and put the cake on a plate.

'Uh-huh. Does your friend take milk and sugar?'

'Yup—two sugars.' He chuckled richly to himself. 'Poor old Nige—he's been absolutely dying to meet you, you know—all the chaps are. You've been voted the official pin-up of first year med.'

'How flattering!' she observed drily. 'How's the course going? Are you enjoying it?'

'It's great!' His eyes, the same amber-brown as her own, lit up. 'Very hard work, but I expected that.'

The smile was replaced just as swiftly by a frown. 'The only thing is, I feel bad about taking an allowance from you. Now I've left school, I should be helping you out, not making it more difficult for you.'

'You're not making it difficult,' she insisted firmly, shifting him aside so that she could reach the drawer that held the cake-knife. 'Besides, this is the reason I wanted you to stay on at school and take your A-levels. If you packed it in now, it would all have been wasted. Anyway, if it makes you feel better, you can look on it as a loan. When you're a world-famous surgeon you can pay me back.'

'That's a promise,' he asserted, snatching a crumb from the plate as she sliced the cake and getting his hand slapped away for his pains. 'Shouldn't that be on one of those doily things?'

'Oh, yes—I forgot. Get one out for me, Ollie—I think she keeps them in the second drawer.'

'What do you think of her latest kick?' he enquired as he went to do as she had asked.

'The tennis?' She laughed. 'Well, as she says, it's good for her, and it gets her out of the house. I don't like to let her sit around moping.'

'Well, she could have found something a little cheaper to take up,' he remarked caustically. 'The membership fees alone for a swanky club like that must cost a fortune, let alone hiring the courts, and taking lessons. And she just expects you to fork out the cash to pay for it all. It's not fair.'

Alysha smiled wryly. 'Oh, I don't mind. Besides, money's not going to be so tight any more. I've...just been offered a big contract by one of the top cosmetic houses. It should pay pretty well.'

'Really? That's great!' Her brother beamed in genuine delight.

She shrugged her slim shoulders. 'Oh, well ... It's no big deal,' she murmured diffidently. 'It's only modelling, after all. Although there's going to be a bit of television work in it, too.'

Ollie's mouth pulled a grim line. 'This isn't really what you wanted out of life, is it, Sis?' he queried with gentle sympathy. 'Modelling, I mean. Look, when I'm finished med school, why don't you go back and finish your veterinary degree? It wouldn't be too late.'

She shook her head, laughing it off. 'I'm afraid it would. My brain's turned to mush through lack of use these past couple of years—I don't think I'd ever be able to go back to the sort of studying I'd need to do to be a vet. Anyway, I'm not so sure I'd want to now. I think I'd like to try something different—maybe even get into television. This contract could be my big chance.'

'Does the Mater know about it?' he enquired with a quirky grin. 'I wouldn't tell her if I were you—if she thinks there's going to be more money around, she'll only go out and spend it.'

'I mentioned it to her.' Alysha smiled in sardonic humour. 'I'm afraid she wasn't nearly so impressed as she was by your first two weeks as a budding doctor.'

He snorted. 'That's only because she wants to be able to say "my son, the doctor". The fact that it's your job that's making it possible tends to escape her. But it doesn't escape me,' he added, his voice low and sincere. 'I really do appreciate it, Sis. I don't think you really know how much.'

'Oh, go on with you,' she protested, chuckling. 'Here, take the cake and go back in the drawing-room and rescue your poor friend. You've left him alone with her all this time—she'll be driving him potty.'

'Lord—poor Nige! I forgot him.' He took up the plate, vanishing swiftly down the passage.

Alysha leaned back against the kitchen table with a sigh. The contract with Ross Elliot was signed; she had sold her soul to him for enough money to keep her family in security for the foreseeable future. Well, strictly speaking, not her soul but her body, she amended, her mouth a little dry. But she couldn't help feeling it rather amounted to the same thing.

CHAPTER THREE

'ALYSHA, this way.'

'Over here, Alysha.'

'Give us a big smile, Alysha.'

'Miss Jones, do you use Lozier products yourself?'

'Of course she does,' Ross cut in before she could frame her own reply to the reporter's question. 'As a model whose career depends on her looks, what else would you expect her to use?'

Alysha kept smiling, though it was taking every ounce of professionalism she possessed. Perched up on a tiny dais with a giant-size mock-up of the Lozier perfume bottle, in front of the gathered media and senior executives of the Lozier company, she felt like a puppet—with Ross Elliot pulling the strings.

Oh, there was no denying that it was a sensational outfit—what little there was of it. Of floating silk chiffon, in a vivid shade of flamingo-pink shot through with gold thread, the top consisted of no more than a wrap of fabric tied halter-style around her neck and across her breasts and knotted behind her back, the two ends drifting to the floor; the palazzo pants were of the same sheer fabric, giving the impression almost of transparency, and they were slung daringly low around her slender hips, leaving most of the peach-smooth curve of her stomach bare—offering a very provocative glimpse of her dainty navel.

But it was in her contract that she had to wear whatever he dictated for her appearances as the Lozier

Girl—as he hadn't hesitated to remind her when she had protested. It said a great deal about the way he saw her, she reflected bitterly: a body, and a face, and twenty-four inches of glossy black hair, that existed solely for the purpose of selling the product. But it was too late now to change her mind about the deal—a substantial proportion of the advance had already been spent on reducing her mother's credit-card accounts and paying her brother's allowance for the term.

The Press conference he had arranged to announce the selection of the new Lozier Girl was being held in the elegant Mayfair offices of the Lozier Institute. It had created quite a stir of interest, even beyond the narrow confines of the advertising and fashion world—one previous Lozier Girl had gone on to become a big success in Hollywood, another had recently married a viscount. Everyone was eager to see who the replacement was to be.

'Will you be doing the Paris collections this year, Alysha?' one of the journalists wanted to know.

Ross nodded, again answering on her behalf. 'Alysha has already been approached by several of the top designers. And of course, her exclusive contract with Lozier doesn't prevent her appearing on the catwalk—or the cover of *Vogue*. Although we do have first call on her services,' he added, slanting her a snake-like smile. 'And we'll be keeping her pretty busy.'

'Do you have a regular boyfriend, Alysha? What does he think of your career?'

'There's no one special at the moment,' she managed to get in before Ross could put words in her mouth.

'Which Lozier preparation is your favourite, Miss Jones?'

Ross glanced towards her; apparently she was to be allowed to answer that one all by herself. Unfortunately he hadn't bothered to check with her before asserting so confidently that she used the range she had been employed to promote—she privately thought it rather over-priced. But of course she couldn't say that—a little prevarication was called for.

'I think a good moisturiser is one of the most important beauty investments a woman can make,' she asserted smilingly.

That bland comment seemed to satisfy them, and the remaining questions were all about the campaign itself, which Ross answered. Some of the photographers wanted more pictures, and she posed obligingly—at least it would be a change to be featured on the editorial pages instead of the fashion section.

At last Ross signalled an end to the proceedings. 'Thank you very much, ladies and gentlemen. There are Press-packs available for you as you leave which I trust will supply you with any further information you may need.'

As the room began to empty, Alysha permitted herself a small sigh of relief, easing the muscles in her back. Ross slanted her a look of sardonic enquiry, offering her his hand to step down from the high dais.

'Tired?'

'Not at all,' she responded coolly, withdrawing her hand from his.

A flicker of a smile curved that hard mouth. 'Good—you have another hour's work still. There are drinks being served in the boardroom for Lozier's senior executives. The chairman tells me he's looking forward very much to meeting you,' he added, allowing his steel gaze to rove without haste over the slender curves of her body: a subtle reminder—if she had needed one—that she had been bought. 'His latest divorce came through a few weeks ago, I believe, so if you play your cards right you could even get to be Lady Maynard the Fourth—or would it be the Fifth? I'm afraid I've lost count.'

Her eyes flashed him a frost-warning, but she chose to ignore his attempts to goad her. This was the first time she had seen him since she had agreed to sign the contract; the respite had been welcome, giving her a chance to sort out her feelings about him.

She couldn't pretend that she didn't *have* any feelings; that spark of physical attraction that arced between them was too real to be ignored. And she knew that he was aware of it too—though he had so far given no indication that he remembered their first meeting; she had wondered whether the sight of so much of her naked flesh would jog his memory, but apparently it hadn't—or if it had, he still chose not to mention it.

The last of the journalists were drifting away. As one of them, from one of the teenage comics—a very self-possessed young woman with improbable copper-red hair and earrings that looked as if they were made from the spare parts of a Harley-Davidson—passed close to the dais she slanted Alysha a look of undisguised contempt.

'"I think a good moisturiser is one of the most important beauty investments a woman can make,"' she mimicked to her companion in a breathy, little-girl voice, clearly intended to be overheard. 'What an air-head!'

Alysha felt herself tense in annoyance; another one who subscribed to that irritating stereotype of the model as a pea-brained clothes-horse! She really ought to have become inured to being treated as if her intelligence quotient was slightly smaller than her dress size by now, but it still stung.

But then, she hadn't been given much opportunity to display anything different, she acknowledged with a touch of asperity—thanks to Ross Elliot. Her role had been made crystal-clear to her—she was simply to look beautiful, and leave the talking to him.

Those perceptive steel-grey eyes noted the flicker that crossed her smooth face, and he smiled with sardonic humour. 'I gather you heard that parting crack,' he remarked drily. 'I shouldn't let it worry you—she's probably profoundly jealous.'

She returned him a coolly level look. 'It doesn't worry me,' she countered. 'But perhaps it should worry you—it can't do Lozier a lot of good to have people think the only women who use their stuff are air-heads. Not the kind of image I should have thought they would want.'

He acknowledged her point with a slight inclination of his head. 'So what do you suggest?' he enquired, a faint edge of mockery in his voice. 'An appearance on *Mastermind*?'

'I don't think it would be necessary to go that far,' she retorted with a touch of asperity. 'Simply allowing me to answer a few questions myself now and then should suffice.'

'I thought I had.'

'Two,' she reminded him pointedly. 'And with one of those I had to lie.'

'Oh?' Those steel-grey eyes glinted a danger-warning. 'And which one was that?'

Her soft mouth took on a sardonic smile—at last she had succeeded in needling him. But as she turned him an aloof shoulder and started to walk away he reached out and caught her arm, forcing her round to face him. 'Which one?' he repeated roughly.

She glared up at him, arching one finely drawn eyebrow in calculated challenge. His fingers were biting into her soft flesh, but she'd be damned if she'd plead with him to let her go—she would never plead with him for anything. 'Why?' she queried, her voice laced with icy disdain. 'Are you jealous?'

He laughed harshly, but released his vice-like grip. 'I've just signed you to a very lucrative contract,' he reminded her. 'I don't have time for some possessive boyfriend objecting to the amount of travelling you'll be required to do. And I don't want you mooning about pining for some lover you've left at home, either.'

A hot surge of anger rose inside her, but she bit down on it hard, merely shrugging her slender shoulders in a gesture of casual dismissal. 'There won't be any problem,' she assured him with haughty dignity.

'I'm very glad to hear it . . .'

'Well now, Ross, come along,' a jovial voice interrupted them. Sir Richard Maynard, chief executive of Lozier Cosmetics, breezed up with Barbara on his arm. 'You can't hog our new Lozier Girl to yourself all the time, you know. If you won't introduce me, I shall have to ask Miss Lange here to do the honours.'

Barbara's fine eyes danced merrily. 'I'm sure you need no introduction, Sir Richard,' she assured him in a soft purr. She was looking stylishly elegant in a beautifully cut business suit of charcoal grey pin-striped worsted, an eye-catching silk scarf chicly knotted at her throat; beside her, Alysha felt by contrast even more underdressed—it was an acutely uncomfortable sensation.

The chairman chuckled, and held out his hand to Alysha. 'I'm delighted to meet you, my dear. You handled that scrum very well—that pretty smile never slipped once. You made a good choice, Ross—an excellent choice.'

Ross conceded a faintly sardonic smile. 'I think so,' he acknowledged. 'Out of all the possible candidates we considered, Miss Jones was the one who most closely matched our requirements.'

'She certainly does. Quite exquisitely beautiful—a veritable work of art!'

Alysha felt her jaw tighten with anger; he was looking at her as if he was planning to add her to his collection. Although she could hardly blame Sir Richard, she acknowledged fairly—it was Ross's fault; this skimpy outfit he had made her wear left so little to the imagination that any red-blooded male would be champing at the bit. Struggling to wrap herself in at least a few shreds of dignity, she tilted up her chin, returning the chairman's handshake firmly.

'Thank you, Sir Richard,' she returned, smiling with a confidence she was far from feeling. 'I'm very happy to be involved in such an exciting campaign.'

'Exciting? Yes, indeed it is,' he agreed, keeping hold of her hand and drawing it through his arm. 'But then we have a reputation to keep up at Lozier's—nothing but the best is good enough, never mind the cost.'

She laughed, though perhaps her merriment was a little forced; but Barbara had taken Ross's attention, and she was conscious of a sudden feeling of deflation that she would have found hard to explain.

'I can't argue with that!' she conceded jaggedly, slanting a covert glance at Ross. A sudden memory had flashed into her mind, a vivid image of her own younger self, in the days when money had seemed to her to grow on trees, standing there with a wad of notes in her hand, offering them to him to pay for the photographic session. She knew better now, of course—top professionals like him just didn't work with amateurs who walked in off the street, no matter what the fee. No wonder he had decided to teach her a lesson . . .

'Well now, let me take you up to the boardroom,' Sir Richard coaxed, seemingly quite unaware that her attention was not focused entirely on himself. 'We have an excellent lunch laid on. I do hope you'll try some of it—you don't have to watch that delightful figure *all* the time, I'm sure!'

'Of course not,' she conceded, managing a smile. 'In fact, I'm quite hungry after that long session this morning.'

'Excellent!'

The boardroom was on the first floor, an elegant salon with wood-panelled walls and a gleaming parquet floor. Alysha hesitated in the doorway; the room was full of senior executives of Lozier Cosmetics, all of them men, all wearing sober grey business suits and serious expressions. But not one of them could apparently control the instinctive swivel of his eyes, nor prevent them lingering in unmistakable concupiscence over the expanse of silken, honeyed flesh so invitingly on display.

At that moment she hated Ross Elliot more acutely than ever. It was bad enough having to pose for photographs wearing such a provocatively revealing outfit—it was far worse to have to walk around in it. It felt as if every man in the room was mentally unfastening the knot in that narrow strip of fabric which covered her breasts, painting in his imagination their firm, pink-tipped ripeness . . .

'Now, what can I get you?' Sir Richard offered genially. 'A little caviar, perhaps?'

'Thank you.' She held herself very erect as they crossed the room, although she was conscious of a profound wish that the floor would open up and swallow her. But Barbara and Ross had followed them up the stairs, and she was determined not to give him the satisfaction of knowing how awful she felt.

A generous buffet had been set out on a long walnut sideboard, served by two white-liveried waiters. Sir Richard pondered the presentation with as serious attention as he would have given a corporate balance sheet, judiciously selecting the choicest dishes.

'So tell me, how long have you been a model, Miss Jones? Or may I call you Alysha?' he enquired, confident of her assent.

She turned on her most dazzling professional smile. 'Almost two years,' she responded, forcing herself to make small-talk as if supremely unaware of the lustful stares of all the other men in the room.

'And you enjoy it?'

'Oh, very much so.' Ross was standing close behind her, talking quietly to Barbara, and Alysha found herself contemplating the sharp prongs of her silver fork—she had never thought of herself as a violent person, but the desire to wipe the smile from that arrogant face was growing more and more powerful by the moment . . .

Sir Richard chuckled, patting her arm in avuncular fashion. 'Well, I'm quite sure we shall enjoy having you as the Lozier Girl,' he assured her. 'I don't think we've ever had a prettier one—isn't that right, Ross?'

She found herself subjected once again to that insolent survey, and a tinge of heat coloured her cheeks; beneath the tight wrap of silk that constrained her breasts she could feel them ripening in an instinctive response that she was powerless to control, the tender nipples so hard that she knew their contours must be clearly visible to him.

'You could be right,' he acceded, the enigmatic glint in his eyes throwing her once again into a turmoil of confusion; surely he must remember . . . ?

'And she's not just a pretty face, you know,' Barbara put in with the generosity of one who was completely confident of her own allure. 'She was studying at university before she decided to become a model. Though I'm very glad she decided on a change of career—she's one of the best girls I've ever had on my books.'

'Really?' Sir Richard looked impressed that the exotic butterfly on his arm could possess more than two brain-cells between her dainty ears. 'What were you studying?'

'I was going to be a vet,' she informed him, conscious of a small glow of satisfaction at the faint look of surprise that flickered across Ross's face.

'And what made you decide to give it up?' Sir Richard enquired.

She shrugged her slender shoulders in a gesture of casual unconcern; she was determined that no one— least of all Ross Elliot—should know the truth. 'Oh, I wanted a little more excitement,' she responded airily. 'It was a five-year course, and it's very demanding—I don't think I quite had the dedication for it.'

Sir Richard chuckled indulgently. 'Quite right. A pretty young thing like you doesn't want to be hiding herself away behind a pile of fusty old books—eh, Ross?'

'It would certainly be a great loss to the world,' he concurred, those steel-grey eyes seeming to mock her.

'Men!' Barbara protested indignantly. 'You all seem to think that if a woman happens to be just halfway attractive, she shouldn't want to do anything more than stand around for you to admire.'

'If she's a model,' Ross pointed out, a sliver of contempt in his voice, 'that's what she's paid for.'

Alysha returned him a glittering glare. 'Well, with all the advances of modern technology, they'll probably have invented a robot that can take over the job in a few years' time,' she remarked caustically.

'Oh, I don't think so,' he responded, his voice softly provocative. 'Technology will have to go a very long way to mimic the silky texture of a woman's skin, the way her body moves ... that fascinating little flutter of her belly as she breathes.'

He was looking levelly into her eyes, but Alysha instantly tensed, holding herself rigid as she tried to prevent that slight tremor in her stomach muscles— she had never even been aware of it until he had mentioned it, but now it seemed to her as if he was accusing her of the most wantonly seductive behaviour.

He saw the blush that suffused her cheeks, and a faint smile of mocking amusement curved that hard mouth. He was doing it deliberately, making her feel even more naked and vulnerable than she already was. Fighting down the seething anger that was bubbling inside her, she turned to Sir Richard.

'This is a wonderful old building,' she remarked, desperately grasping at any topic of conversation to turn the focus from herself and her physical attributes. 'One of the original houses of the Grosvenor Estate, isn't it?'

He looked a little bemused by her question, but responded gallantly. 'Why... yes, I believe it is—although I'm afraid the interior has been considerably remodelled over the years. Perhaps you'd like to see the rest of the building?' he added, the honeyed note in his voice warning her that his offer probably included rather more than an architectural tour.

'I'd love to,' she responded, keeping her smile in place while mentally vowing to do no such thing. 'But first, could I have a piece of that strawberry pavlova? I'm afraid it's one of my weaknesses.'

'Of course, my dear. What a pleasure to find a girl with such a healthy appetite—so many of them these days seem just to pick at their food...'

To Alysha's relief, with that manoeuvre she had succeeded in detaching herself from Ross; though as Sir Richard scooped a generous helping of Pavlova on to her plate she couldn't help slanting a covert glance across the room.

Barbara was still at Ross's side. That would create more fuel for the gossips, Alysha reflected, aware of an odd little twinge of something she didn't care to analyse too closely. There had been a lot of speculation over the past couple of weeks; it was no secret that the two of them had been seen together on several occasions, at the theatre or dining *tête-à-tête* in some exclusive restaurant.

They made quite a striking couple, she was forced to concede; his air of faintly hard-edged cynicism was a perfect foil for her charm and sophistication. From time to time Barbara would make some small gesture—touching his arm to emphasise a point, brushing a speck of dust from his lapel—that sent out an unmistakable message: these two were lovers.

It should really be no surprise that they had got back together—after all, they were both very attractive people, and they had a great deal in common. Perhaps that was why Ross had never settled down, had earned himself such a reputation for transitory relationships—perhaps it had been Barbara he had loved all along.

Meanwhile, Sir Richard was offering her that most flattering attention. Maybe it was a little unwise to appear to be responding quite so readily, to laugh so freely at his thin jokes; but his open admiration was a balm for her bruised spirits. And she felt a good deal safer with him than she would have with Ross— at least he was a gentleman.

She was scheduled to remain at the reception until two, and although the hands on the splendid mahogany long-case clock beside the door seemed to be creeping round dreadfully slowly, each time she looked they were a little closer to the magic hour.

At the sound of the first chime, she turned to Sir Richard with a smile of sweet regret. 'I'm afraid I have to go now.'

'Already?' he protested, glancing at the clock.

'I was only due to stay until two o'clock,' she reminded him demurely. 'I have to be somewhere else.'

He lifted one greying eyebrow in mild surprise that anything could be more important than remaining at his side, but conceded a smile, patting her arm. 'All right then, you'd better run along. But I wonder if you have anything planned for tomorrow night? I'd very much like to take you out to dinner.'

She hesitated, careful to pick her words—the last thing she wanted was to alienate the chairman of the company who had signed up her services for the next three years, with an option on a further two. But she couldn't afford to risk leading him on, either.

'I'm . . . sorry—I'm going away this weekend.'

'One day next week then, perhaps?'

She shook her head. 'I don't really think it will be possible.'

'Ah—I see . . .' He nodded, smiling. 'Of course, I quite understand. How very silly of me not to realise that a lovely thing like you would already be spoken for. Well, I can only say he's a very lucky fellow. But nevertheless, it's been delightful meeting you, my dear—quite delightful.'

He lifted her hand to his lips in a gesture of old-fashioned gallantry, but then before she had realised what he was going to do he had pulled her against him and was kissing her on the cheek in a far from avuncular fashion. She stiffened, but she had no choice but to tolerate his embrace—she could hardly create a scene here in the crowded board-room by pushing him away.

He let her go at last, and with smile that she hoped concealed her considerable relief she slipped out of his arms, and escaped from the room.

She had left her own clothes in the office of the secretary to the sales director, on the top floor. There was a lift, but the stairs were nearer, and she ran nimbly up them. She had almost reached the top when she stumbled, losing one flimsy high-heeled sandal, which tumbled back down to the landing below.

'Drat!' She started down to fetch it, but just as she reached the bottom of the flight she heard someone else coming up—and as he turned the corner she found herself face to face with Ross. Instinct would have had her run, but she could hardly do that with dignity, so she stood her ground.

He stooped and picked up the shoe, holding it out to her, a faintly sardonic smile curving that hard mouth. 'Here you are, Cinderella,' he teased provocatively. 'You're running away in quite a hurry. Not enjoying the ball?'

'It's two o'clock,' she pointed out, holding herself stiffly erect, conscious of an uncomfortable feeling of vulnerability in this skimpy costume and with one teetering heel throwing her off balance. 'That's the time I'm entitled to leave.'

'And you seemed to be getting along so well with Sir Richard,' he derided. 'Or are you playing hard to get? You're probably wise—he's a sly old buzzard. He might have been drooling over you as if he was ready to drop into the palm of your hand, but if you want to get a ring on your finger you'll have to use a little strategy.'

Her eyes flashed him a frost warning. 'For your information,' she informed him, her voice as cold as polar ice, 'I've no interest whatsoever in marrying Sir Richard—nor anyone else, for that matter. I don't regard my career as a mere stepping-stone to finding a rich husband—I intend to make my own success. Besides,' she added, unable to restrain herself, 'I'm surprised you had time to notice what I was doing with Sir Richard. It seemed to me that Barbara was hogging your attention to the exclusion of all else.'

He laughed in lazy mockery. 'Ah, so that's what's been bugging you,' he taunted. '*You're* jealous.'

She caught herself up, her cheeks flushing a vivid shade of pink as she tried to shrug off his arrogant accusation. 'Jealous? Of course not—that's ridiculous.' She snatched her sandal from his hand, and turned to continue up the stairs, her head tilted at a haughty angle. But he caught one of the trailing ends of her skimpy top, halting her escape.

'Oh, yes, you are,' he insisted, his voice laced with biting sarcasm. 'You're one of those women who can't be happy unless she has every man she meets panting on the end of a leash, aren't you? Well, I'm afraid you're wasting your time with me—I'm not the type to be any woman's tame poodle. Though if it makes you feel good,' he added, his eyes sliding down over the slender curves of her body in a way that made her go hot all over, 'I'll admit I wouldn't kick you out of bed.'

'I . . . Whatever makes you think you'd ever get the chance?' she challenged, the racing of her heartbeat belying her defiant words; he was slowly winding the long tie around his hand, reeling her inexorably towards him against all her efforts to hold back. 'You're the *last* person I'd ever want to go to bed with.'

Those steel-grey eyes glinted with sardonic amusement. 'What a toffee-nosed little bitch you are,' he murmured tauntingly. 'You really can't bring yourself to admit that there's nothing you'd like better than a nice rough tussle with a misbred mongrel like me.'

That intriguing mouth had curved into a cruel, sensual smile, and she felt herself mesmerised. He was going to kiss her again . . .

'The Sir Richards of this world are all very well,' he growled, his voice low and husky, 'but it would be nothing less than a sin to waste that sweet, tender young body on a rich old man with cold, crabby hands. You need someone whose hands are warm . . .'

His own slid around her slim waist, burning the naked flesh like a brand. She stiffened, trying to draw back, but with an abrupt jerk he dragged her ruthlessly into his arms. He was holding the knot of her top, tightening it in a way that crushed her tender breasts, and she knew from the warning intent in his eyes that at the slightest attempt to struggle he would drag it up over them, leaving them naked.

And so she could only submit as his head bent over hers, and his lips brushed her mouth, firm and warm, tantalising. Her jaw was clamped rigid in resistance, but the challenge in that merely seemed to provoke him. Very slowly and deliberately he traced the outline of her trembling lips with the hot tip of his tongue, flickering it between them, seeking out the sensitive corners, probing in a flagrantly sensual exploration that was rapidly undermining all her defences.

And then he took hold of the full curve of her lower lip between his teeth, nipping at it delicately, and she gasped as a *frisson* of heat shivered through her. He took immediate advantage of her parted lips, his tongue swirling in to plunder the sweet, moist depths of her mouth, tasting his fill.

She couldn't help herself; she was melting instinctively into his hard embrace, every inch of her supple body curved against his. With every ragged breath the tight constraint of the silk over her breasts was a delicious torment, rasping at her delicate nipples until they hardened to raw buds, the exquisite focus of a million sweet sensations. She was aching for his caress, and as she felt his hand stroke up over the smooth curve of her stomach with unmistakable intent she moaned softly, moving in unconscious invitation, wantonly abandoning all the promises she had made to herself about not letting him do this to her...

Somewhere a door opened, and the sound of voices drifted up to her—footsteps approaching. Startled into finding her strength, she pushed him away, her cheeks flaming with embarrassment as three of the grey-suited executives appeared around the bend of the stairs, their expressions of surprise turning quickly to conspiratorial male amusement as they guessed exactly what had been happening.

She turned and fled, stumbling slightly on the stairs, Ross's mocking laughter pursuing her as she made her escape.

CHAPTER FOUR

'I DON'T believe I'm doing this. I really don't believe I'm doing this.'

Alysha closed her eyes briefly, but when she opened them the scene was exactly the same. She was walking the wrong way down the middle of one of the busiest streets in the centre of Bangkok, with several lanes of traffic streaming past her on either side, barefoot and wearing a vividly multi-coloured bikini-top with a matching sarong slung low around her hips, and a large straw hat on her head—and holding two half-grown leopard cubs on the end of a long leather leash.

'That's great, Alysha—terrific! Look cool, now.'

'Cool?' she protested indignantly. 'This tarmac's practically melting! My feet feel like a couple of overcooked steaks!'

It was only a little past nine-thirty, but the hot sun was blazing down from a brilliantly blue sky, sparkling on the vivid green and orange pagoda roofs of the Grand Palace behind her. They had been shooting for over two hours, and in all that time the traffic hadn't abated for even so much as a minute—where were all these people *going*? The relentless noise was making her head ache, and she could almost taste the diesel fumes that hung like a grey pall in the air.

When she had first learned what they intended for this shot, she had taken some convincing that the cubs would come to no harm from it. But their trainer was clearly as concerned for their welfare as she was, insisting on regular breaks for them, and they seemed quite oblivious of the traffic around them, straining forward towards the lure of raw meat he was dragging in front of them, just below camera-range.

Drawing in a long, deep breath she focused her attention again to obey the director's shouted instructions, letting her hips sway with a slight swagger as she strolled towards the camera.

'I don't believe in dicing with danger,' she purred. 'When I go out in the sun. I always protect myself.'

They had attracted quite an audience, tourists and local people gathered along the pavements and on the footbridge that crossed the busy road to watch them. It was quite a circus; half a dozen assorted vehicles, several tons of equipment and a four-man film crew, as well as Harry Keaton and his two photographic assistants, the location manager, the hairdresser, the fashion stylist—and Alastair, the cosmetics genius, who had become den-mother to the whole ill-matched bunch.

And that wasn't all—up on the footbridge that spanned the seven-lane road was a second camera crew, filming the making of the commercial for an hour-long television special. That was a small bombshell Ross had dropped on her three days before she had left for Thailand. The camera crew were following her everywhere, watching as she was made-up, watching her eat—she was never off duty.

There was a momentary lull as the traffic-lights up ahead changed to let the queue piling up in the sidestreet emerge. Lorries and tankers, chromed taxis and open-backed trishaws, mopeds piled high with goods to be delivered, surged out, to be directed around the obstruction in the middle of the road by a white-uniformed policeman with a piercing whistle. Not that they seemed to take much notice of him; from time to time he would get really agitated, gesticulating wildly to apparently no effect whatsoever, as the traffic streamed by around him with minimal consideration for the basic courtesy of the road.

Quite how Ross had negotiated permission for them to take over the centre of town like this she wasn't quite certain—presumably it was the value to the vital tourist trade that had been the incentive. They had been here for almost a week, and each day's shooting had been more outrageous than the last—yesterday she had spent reclining languidly on a pile of cushions in one of the long, shallow 'longtail' boats, a beautifully-marked python coiled elegantly around her arms and the tall, graceful spires of the Temple of the Dawn in the background, being filmed from a low-flying helicopter which had created so much turbulence that she had been terrified she was going to be tipped out into the blue-grey waters of the Chao Phraya river.

It was certainly going to be a spectacular campaign; of course she had known that her face was going to become famous, but she was just beginning to realise *how* famous—once the billboards started to appear, it was going to be difficult for her even to walk down the street without being recognised. Life was never going to be quite the same again.

'OK, folks, just one more take,' the director of the television commercial called. 'Then we can all relax.'

There was a brief flurry of activity as the shot was set up again—the leopard cubs' trainer insisted they needed a drink of water, Alastair darted out from the camper-van he used as his studio to dust her nose and cheeks lightly with translucent powder—and then she took her place, ready to repeat that one brief sequence of action for what felt like the hundredth time.

Suddenly a familiar silhouette up on the footbridge caught her eye, and she felt her heartbeat give an odd little thud. So Ross had arrived. He had said he would be coming out, but she had had no idea when. Had Barbara come with him? The gossip-machine was still buzzing with rumours—but then you shouldn't believe everything you heard.

Well, he couldn't complain about how hard she was working, she reflected with a touch of asperity. She had been up at five every morning, to spend over an hour being made-up and dressed before starting work by seven—and then after a break during the middle of the day, starting again at about four and going on until seven in the evening.

'Is everyone ready?' the director called. 'OK then, sweetheart, off you go.'

The man's patronising manner was becoming more irritating with every session, but Alysha's professionalism enabled her to maintain her poise. It was less easy to forget that Ross was there, watching her from up on the footbridge, those steel-grey eyes missing nothing; impossible to forget the way he had kissed her . . .

'I don't believe in dicing with danger . . .'

At last it was over. The animal trainer darted forward to take the cubs off to their cage, and she was able to retreat into the cool of the air-conditioned camper-van. With a sigh of relief she handed her straw hat over to Gemma, and threw herself out full-length on the comfortable bench-seat along the back, stretching her arms above her head and closing her eyes.

'Thank goodness for that! If I'd had to stay out there another minute, I'd have melted into a puddle on the tarmac.'

'We couldn't go on shooting—the light's starting to bleach out the colours,' Ross pointed out with crisp indifference as he stepped up into the camper behind her.

She opened her eyes a slit to glitter a silent malediction at him, and groaned as she saw the documentary crew about to follow him in. 'Can't I have a break from that bunch for a while?' she pleaded irritably, sitting up. 'They've done everything but film me taking a shower!'

He glanced down at her, one dark eyebrow lifted in unsympathetic query, but turned back to the crew, dispatching them with a brief word.

'Thank you,' she conceded, closing her eyes again.

'I warned you it was going to be hard work,' he reminded her with a total lack of compassion. 'I hope you're not going to flake out on me.'

'Of course I won't,' she retorted indignantly. 'But it's been six days now, working every day in this heat— I think I'm entitled to feel just a little frazzled.'

'Take no notice of him—he's a sadistic slave-driver,' Alastair advised trenchantly, elbowing Ross unceremoniously out of the way to bring her a glass of his speciality reviver, an exotic blend of fruit-juices made to his own secret recipe. It was fresh from the fridge, dewy with moisture, and she wiped it soothingly across her hot forehead before taking a sip.

Ross laughed drily. 'I've got a campaign to bring in on schedule—and don't forget the whole crew are on a bonus if we make it.'

The older man pursed his lips and shrugged his thin shoulders. 'So? Money isn't everything,' he asserted with exaggerated dignity.

Ross's hard mouth twitched with genuine amusement. 'I've never seen you working for nothing,' he countered.

From the bench, Alysha watched the exchange with covert interest. Alastair was the only person she had ever heard dare to speak to Ross like that—but he didn't seem to be annoyed. No doubt it was one of the privileges of being accounted an eccentric genius, to be able to get away with things no one else could— but at least it proved that Ross really did possess a sense of humour after all. It was an intriguing revelation . . .

Hey, don't start thinking you could like the guy, she warned herself swiftly. Remember what he did to you.

How could she forget? Every time she was even in the same room with him, she felt that same quivering vulnerability, as if she was again half-naked, even when she was fully dressed—she had to force herself not to yield to that instinctive urge to lift her hands to cover her breasts.

He was checking through the shooting schedule, and seemed satisfied as he tossed the clipboard down on a table. 'Well, people, you'll be pleased to know you can all have a day off tomorrow,' he announced to the assembled company.

A weary cheer went up from the floor, where most of the others were sprawled, sipping cans of ice-cold lager. 'Right—I'm going to check out the local night-life,' declared Doug, the photographer's assistant.

'I've been here a week, and not so much as a sniff of action.'

'It's the pool for me,' Gemma announced, slanting a provocative glance in Ross's direction. 'I've bought a brand-new bikini, and I haven't even got it wet yet.'

He lifted one dark eyebrow in indulgent amusement. 'Really? I shall be sorry to miss that—unfortunately I'm going to be busy for the best part of the day.'

Doug nudged her, chuckling lewdly. 'Never mind, Gem,' he snickered. 'Tell you what, why don't you hit the town with me tonight, and then we can both sleep it off by the pool tomorrow?'

She returned him a look of withering scorn. 'Not in your wildest dreams,' she countered caustically.

Doug shrugged, untroubled by the expected rebuff. 'Ah, well—it was worth a try.'

Alysha joined in the general laughter. The atmosphere on this shoot was typical of most location trips she had been on. She and Gemma were the only two women, and from the moment they had arrived most of the men had been jockeying against each other for their attention, playing silly little games of one-upmanship—except for Alastair, of course, and Harry Keaton, who seemed interested only in his cameras. And Ross.

It was all no more than good-natured fun—one of the first things she had learned when she had started modelling was how to maintain just sufficient distance to get the message across that she wasn't interested in bed-hopping games, and though she knew some people regarded her as rather stand-offish no one seemed to mind.

The only person on this trip that she didn't seem able to get along with was Gemma—did she regard all models with that faintly supercilious disdain, or was it just her? 'I think I'll join you by the pool,' she remarked, trying to strike a friendly note. 'I can't think of a better way to spend a day.'

'Mind you don't catch the sun,' Alastair reminded her quickly. 'It'll take hours if we have to do body make-up.'

'Alysha won't have time to sit in the sun,' Ross cut in. 'She's coming out with me.'

'What?' She glanced up at him in alarm, 'Where?'

'Sightseeing.' A flicker of sardonic amusement crossed his face. 'The Grand Palace, among other things. With the documentary crew.'

'No!' Her eyes flashed in angry defiance. 'Why should I? I'm entitled to a rest too.'

'It's part of our agreement with the Thai Tourist Board,' he responded, coolly indifferent to her arguments. 'That's why we're getting so much co-operation from the authorities—we can't afford to jeopardise it.'

'Oh, great—wonderful!' she sighed, her voice taut with annoyance. 'Are you sure you wouldn't like a couple of pints of my blood as well?'

'I don't think it'll be necessary to go that far,' he responded with a smile of grim humour.

Alysha could think of nothing sufficiently cutting to say to him; if she had had anything suitable in her hands she would have thrown it at him, but her glass wasn't empty, and she'd be damned if she'd waste a drop of Alastair's delicious fruit-cup on such a ... despicable rat! She had to content herself with turning him an aloof shoulder, and proceeding pointedly to ignore him.

Alysha had been longing for a chance to see the Grand Palace—although she would have preferred not to have gone with Ross. She had bought a guidebook in London, and had pored in fascination over the pictures of temples and courtyards, and the magnificent golden throne of the Emerald Buddha.

She had grown accustomed to rising early, while the day was still cool, and it was barely half-past eight when they arrived in the documentary crew's transit van outside the Viseschaisri Gate. But before they could go in, the director decided that it would be fun to inject a little local colour by getting a shot of them arriving in one of Bangkok's notorious motorised trishaws.

It took quite a while for him to select the one that suited him—the most gaudily painted, decked out in tinsel and fur tails like a demented golf-cart—and even longer to negotiate with the excitable driver a price for him to make a brief circuit round the block and back to this spot for the cameras.

Finally invited to take her place on the plastic bench-seat in the back, Alysha eyed the flimsy vehicle with some misgiving—it was completely open, with only a shiny chrome side-rail to protect her from the busy traffic, and nothing to keep out the fug of exhaust fumes in the air.

'Madame, your carriage awaits,' Ross prompted with what she could only construe as gleeful malice.

'I'm sure this isn't in my contract,' she hissed in a biting undertone as she flashed him a glittering smile for the benefit of the cameras.

'Oh, I can assure you it is,' he responded. 'Clause twelve—public relations. Anyway, what are you afraid of? It isn't dangerous—you don't think I'd risk damaging the merchandise at this stage of the campaign, do you?'

'Why not?' she countered caustically. 'I'm quite sure you'd have it well covered by insurance.'

'Of course. But it would cause a serious delay to have to look for a substitute, and ship the whole crew out here again—and I always like to deliver on time.'

She flashed him a frosty glare; he probably wasn't joking. To him, she *was* just a piece of merchandise; and though he had admitted that he wouldn't kick her out of bed, his desire for her was no more than a transitory, physical thing—merely an itch that could be as easily relieved by any other passably attractive female.

The tuk-tuk jerked away from the kerb, swinging out across the lanes of traffic with death-defying disregard for the laden lorry that was coming up behind them. Alysha gasped, grabbing for the side-rail with one hand and Ross's arm with the other—encountering hard, male muscle beneath warm, sun-bronzed skin. She snatched it away at once, her heart pounding even harder.

Ross laughed softly, sliding his arm around her shoulders and drawing her close against him. 'Don't you think this would make a good shot for the cameras?' he taunted, nuzzling into her hair. 'And a nice little sub-plot to make the documentary a little more interesting.'

She pulled herself firmly from his grasp, holding herself stiffly away from him. 'I am *not* going to pretend I'm having an affair with you just for the sake of your damned documentary,' she warned him fiercely.

'No? Pity.' He shrugged his wide shoulders in a gesture of indifference, a glint of provocative amusement lurking in the depths of those steel-grey eyes, but he moved his arm. 'Let's just admire the scenery, then, shall we? I'm relying on you to tell me all about this palace, you know—I'm sure you've been swotting up on all the local culture.'

The sardonic note in his voice stung almost as much as the fact that he was right. 'I've got a guidebook,' she conceded tautly. 'As a matter of fact, it's very interesting. The palace was begun in the 1780s by King Rama I, the ancestor of the present king.'

'Is that the one who was in *The King and I*?'

'No, it wasn't—that was Rama IV,' she retorted. 'And it wasn't at all an accurate picture of him in that film—he was a very intelligent man, and he did a great deal of good for the country.'

'Really? You are a mine of information,' he drawled lazily. 'I suppose you know what all those spires are sticking up over the wall?'

She slanted him a glance of sharp suspicion; he was mocking her with this pretence of ignorance—she already knew he had been to Bangkok a number of times, and she was quite sure he knew as much about the royal palace as she did. 'They're chedi,' she responded tartly. 'The golden one is the Royal Reliquary—it's the biggest golden chedi in the world. The others are... I'm not sure. I think one of them is filled with statues of the kings of Thailand.'

'That sounds exciting,' he remarked, yawning.

She slanted him a look of glittering disdain. 'You were the one who wanted to know,' she bit out.

Those steel-grey eyes glinted with sardonic humour. 'So I was,' he conceded. 'Carry on. Tell me about this Emerald Buddha.'

She hesitated, eyeing him warily, reluctant to give him another opportunity to taunt her. 'It isn't made of emerald—it's jade. No one knows exactly when it was made—it was found in 1464, in Chiang Rai, up in the far northern provinces. The legend goes that a party of travelling monks got caught in a storm and took shelter in a local temple, when a lightning bolt hit it, revealing the statue.'

He lifted one dark eyebrow in genuine interest. 'What a very romantic story.'

'Yes, it is. Almost too romantic to be true,' she added wryly. 'I mean, doesn't it all seem a bit too convenient—it was a really remote region in those days, and yet a party of important monks just happened to be in the right place at the right time?'

'Cynic,' he teased, chuckling. 'That's supposed to be my line.'

Alysha couldn't help responding with a smile—and it was that expression which the documentary crew's camera caught as the tuk-tuk slewed back into the kerb. Which of course was exactly what Ross had wanted, she admitted to herself with a touch of angry resentment—and as usual he had managed to get his own way.

He climbed out of the tuk-tuk, and gave her a hand to step down on to the pavement, careful not to place himself between her and the camera. 'Thank you,' she acknowledged, excessively gracious.

'Don't mention it.'

She would have pulled her hand away, as usual, but with an almost imperceptible tightening of his fingers he held the grip a little longer than was strictly necessary, those smoky grey eyes smiling down into hers. A strange fluttering had stirred in the pit of her stomach; it was unsettling that, in spite of her mistrust of him, she could never be quite immune to that pernicious charm . . .

'That's great, people—smashing. OK, shall we move along inside the palace now?'

The voice of the director shattered the spell like shards of glass; it had only ever been an illusion, after all—another scene in the documentary of the trip, a little touch of human interest. Summoning every ounce of will-power she possessed, Alysha rearranged her smiling mask, no hint of the turmoil inside her showing on her serene face.

At least she had no need to feign her interest in the sight of all those tapering pagoda roofs and tall chedis, rising above the crenellated white walls that ran all around the palace. If only that damned film crew weren't there, constantly intrusive, drawing attention to her, making everyone turn and stare and wonder who she was.

But once they had bought their tickets, and walked through the archway into the palace compound, she was instantly captivated. The first sight that met her eyes was the two towering mythological giants that guarded the entrance, clad in gilded armour, their fearsome white faces glaring down on all intruders.

'Wow!' She laughed a little uncertainly. 'I wouldn't like to run into them on a dark night.'

'Quite something, aren't they?' Ross agreed, stepping closer to examine the intricate decoration on the traditional-style armour. 'The workmanship in this is just incredible.'

There was so much to see, it was hard to decide which way to walk first. It was all so colourful, a dense forest of temples and reliquaries, of miniature gardens and strange, exotic figures, of golden towers and walls decorated with intricate mosaics of tiny porcelain chips, brightly painted. There was music, too—the tinkling of *gamelan* cymbals, and the soft rhythmic chanting of devout Buddhists at their meditations— and the sweet, heady fragrance of incense drifting on the warm air.

Alysha forgot her irritation, barely even aware of the camera's eye following her around—amid the crowds they were almost unnoticeable, just another group with a video-camera and a tape-recorder, and few people seemed aware that they were doing anything other than filming the beauties of the palace.

The Emerald Buddha itself was housed in the largest of the buildings, a spectacular edifice with green-tiled pagoda roofs and golden pillars, and a wide marble step leading up to the ornately decorated entrance. In the courtyard before it were piled great mounds of offerings—baskets of the choicest fruit and vegetables, ripe and colourful, beautifully arranged— while groups of monks in saffron robes, their heads shaven, squatted on the ground in their devotions, oblivious to the gaping hordes of tourists thronging around them.

They were fortunate to find that they had visited on a day the chapel was open, and they were able go inside, leaving their shoes—and the camera crew—at the door. Inside it was cool and shadowy; at once the atmosphere of quiet and serenity seemed to envelop them—they could have been a million miles away from the hot streets and teeming traffic of Bangkok.

'Do you want to sit down for a while?' Ross asked her in a low voice.

She nodded, tucking her long legs beneath her as everyone else did so as not to point her feet at the sacred figure enthroned on its high golden altar. 'It's smaller than I expected,' she whispered back as he sat down beside her, 'but I don't think I've ever seen anything so beautiful in all my life.'

'Look at the delicacy of that gold filigree-work around the base of the altar,' he murmured. 'There must have been real dedication in the craftsmanship that went into that.'

'All that gold—it must be worth a fortune! It doesn't seem quite right, somehow, in a country where there's so much poverty.'

He shook his head in disagreement. 'That's a very western way of looking at it,' he argued. 'Most Thais are Buddhists. They believe that the position they were born into in this life is the result of their actions in their past lives, and they're happy with it—they just hope that by living well they'll get something better in their next reincarnation. In the meantime, spirituality is very important to them—as it is to everyone, whichever God you believe in or even if you believe in none at all. That's why even all these gawking tourists, when they come in here, sit down on the floor and talk in whispers—they can feel it too.'

She glanced around, and realised that he was right. Whatever it was, there was something powerful here, something that stilled the hurrying mind and brought a sense of pure calm and peacefulness to even the most stressed individual.

But it was a surprise that Ross Elliot should have been aware of it; she had had him down as a tough-minded materialist, only interested in the kind of fast money that could be made in the advertising business. But his photographs had always revealed something more than that, she mused reflectively—a perceptiveness, an artistry... He was a complex character, far deeper than she had initially believed.

Sitting so close to him on the floor, she could feel the warmth emanating from his body, stirring memories that were almost physical of the way he had held her in his arms, the way he had kissed her. There seemed to be nothing she could do to thrust the unwelcome images aside; they were welling up inside her, stirring the ashes of a desire she had always tried to convince herself had been no more than an adolescent infatuation.

But she was no longer an adolescent—she was a woman, and the hunger had grown and matured with her into full-blown, adult craving, an obsession that could only be alleviated in one way. Alleviated—or inflamed: which? There was only one way to find out—but that was a very dangerous path to tread. She wasn't sure she had the courage for it.

And what about Barbara? An uncomfortable stab of guilt made her squirm. How could she even consider letting herself get involved with him? Barbara had done so much for her—she had come to regard her as more of a friend than an agent. It would be the most appalling disloyalty.

And besides, did she really want to get involved with a man like that? He seemed to have very little respect for women—he just used them, and when he had had enough of one relationship he simply moved on to the next, with no compunction whatsoever about the hurt he caused.

She had to hold on to that thought, she vowed with a determination that bordered on desperation—at least it might harden her defences a little. Because it was becoming increasingly difficult to feel confident that if he *did* decide to try to take their relationship beyond the boundaries she had set herself she would be able to resist him.

CHAPTER FIVE

AFTER the searing heat of the Bangkok streets, the lapis-tiled swimming-pool on the terrace of the hotel was a very tempting prospect. Alysha took a quick shower and changed into a sleek fuchsia-pink swimsuit, and then, slipping a loose white shirt on over the top, she dropped a book and some suntan lotion into a straw beach-bag, and made her way back downstairs.

Most of the crew were already there, lounging beneath the shade of the large thatched parasols that surrounded the pool, sipping iced lager from tall frosted glasses. As she approached, some of them glanced up, and she thought she detected a hint of a snigger.

'Hi—had a good time?' Gemma asked in what Alysha felt was just a fraction too sweet a tone.

'Yes, thank you,' she responded guardedly. 'It was very interesting.'

She settled herself on a vacant sun-lounger. A slim young Thai waiter appeared discreetly on cue, and she ordered one of the delicious iced sorbets that were a speciality of the hotel—that would be quite enough to keep her going until dinnertime. She put her book down beside her, but didn't open it—it would seem horribly stand-offish to start to read as soon as she sat down.

'Have you . . . been to Bangkok before?' she asked Gemma, struggling to make conversation; she usually

got on very well with the women she worked with—
after all, they were all there to do a job of work, and
most of them accepted that her looks were simply the
tools of her trade.

The other girl raised a sardonic eyebrow in response. 'Of course—several times.'

'Great place,' Doug grunted from beneath the straw
sun-hat that covered his face. 'Shame about the
traffic.'

'Oh, but if it weren't for that, it would be a lovely
city,' Alysha protested. 'We went on a boat trip
around the canals on the other side of the river this
afternoon, after we'd been to the Grand Palace—it
was really fascinating. All those wooden houses right
on the water—and the people were so friendly, waving
to us as we went by.'

She knew she was gabbling, but she hoped no one
would guess the reason. She had just caught sight of
Ross, strolling towards them around the edge of the
pool; he was wearing a pair of torn-off chinos as
shorts, and a faded, sleeveless blue T-shirt that had
trouble stretching across the width of his well-muscled
shoulders—and he seemed quite unaware of the stir
of feminine interest that followed his lazy progress.

'They were building a temple, too—just like the old
ones in the Grand Palace, with those pointed pagoda-
style roofs,' she rushed on breathlessly. 'They put so
much work into them—it must take ages to do all
those mosaics, with such tiny pieces of china.'

'Sounds like you had a fabulous time,' Gemma
commented drily.

'Yes, I . . . did . . .' A shadow fell across the stone
flags beside her, and her words dried up.

'Hello, everyone,' Ross greeted them with a laconic smile. 'Enjoying your day off?'

There was general assent, except from Doug. 'Don't speak to me about enjoyment,' he grumbled plaintively. 'I'm suffering from the most expensive hangover in history.'

Ross laughed without sympathy. 'If you get drunk in Patpong, what do you expect?' he enquired. 'How much did it cost you?'

'Close to a hundred and fifty quid—just for a few measly drinks and a floor-show. Mind you, what some of those girls can do...! There was one who——'

'Yes, thank you, Doug—I don't think we need the graphic details,' Ross cut him off, a glint of dark humour in his eyes. He slanted a look of surprise at Alysha's sorbet as the waiter brought it to her. 'Ice-cream?'

'Why not?' she responded, taking a spoonful of the delicious, fruit-laden dessert.

'Rather a lot of calories in it, aren't there?' he queried, one dark eyebrow lifted in lazy mockery.

She shrugged her slender shoulders in a gesture of cool indifference. 'I wouldn't know—I never bother counting.'

'No?' There was a note of husky amusement in his voice. 'How do you keep that enticing body in such great shape, then?'

She felt her cheeks flush a deep shade of pink; he was deliberately trying to provoke her, talking like that in front of the others, letting his eyes rove over her in that intimate way. 'I do ballet exercises,' she countered stiffly.

'Ballet, eh?' His hard mouth quirked into a sardonic smile which eloquently conveyed his opinion on the subject. 'It figures.' With a lazy movement he peeled his T-shirt off over his head. 'That water looks good—I think I'll take a swim.'

Alysha was still smarting from the casual derision in his words. She tried not to let her eyes be drawn towards him, but she couldn't help herself—and the sight of that hard-muscled body, the skin lightly bronzed by the sun, made her mouth go dry. There was a thick pelt of rough, dark hair across his wide chest, narrowing into a single line over his lean stomach before disappearing into the waistband of his shorts... Suddenly it was difficult to breathe.

He glanced up, catching her watching him, but she couldn't look away—and the glint of dark mockery in those steel-grey eyes warned her that he knew exactly what effect he was having on her. With slow deliberation, he let his hands drop to the top snap of his shorts, holding her helplessly in the grip of a mesmerising spell.

Of course she knew that he would be wearing something beneath them—but all the same she couldn't prevent the deep flush of colour that swept into her cheeks as her over-heated imagination conjured wild visions of male nakedness. The taut black swimming-trunks did little to cool the fever; it took every ounce of will-power she possessed to force herself to look away.

'Not swimming?' he enquired, a lilt of provocative humour in his voice.

'Not... yet. Maybe in a little while,' she managed to respond.

He taunted her with a knowing smile, then turned away from her, diving smoothly into the water, his dark hair slicked back like a seal's as he broke the surface halfway across the pool and began to swim with lazy, powerful strokes.

Alysha picked up her book, her hands shaking slightly as she found her page. Gemma laughed. 'Tasty, isn't he?' she enquired.

Alysha glanced up enquiringly, her features schooled now into blank indifference. 'Who?'

But the other girl wasn't fooled. 'Oh, come on—you were practically drooling over him just now. They were running a sweepstake before you came down, you know,' she added with a hint of smug humour.

'Oh?'

'On how long it'll take him to get you into bed.'

Alysha almost choked.

'Some of them reckon he's done it already,' Gemma went on with malicious relish. 'But somehow I don't think so. I know that look in his eyes—it usually means he's still enjoying the hunt. Like most men, once he's got what he wants, he starts to lose interest pretty rapidly. I doubt if you'll hold out for long, though,' she added with a superior smile. 'I give it two days—three at the outside.'

'I'm afraid you've got it wrong,' Alysha countered stiffly. 'I have no intention . . . I don't find . . . It isn't like that at all.'

Gemma snickered derisively. 'Oh, don't try to kid me. He has whoever he wants—all he has to do is snap his fingers. You won't be any different from all the rest.'

Alysha forced herself to breathe slowly in and out to steady the racing thud of her heartbeat. 'And I suppose that includes you?' she enquired, her voice taut.

'Of course,' the other girl responded flippantly. 'Oh, it's three or four years ago now—we were on a shoot in . . . Barbados, I think it was. And before you ask—yes, he's great in bed. The best. So long as you can accept that it's only going to be for a couple of weeks or so.'

'He's had longer relationships than that,' Alysha felt compelled to point out.

Gemma shrugged her slim shoulders in a gesture of casual dismissal. 'Not many—three months is about his limit. Of course, every one thinks at the start that it'll be different with her, that *she'll* be the one to make him change his mind about settling down, but it isn't going to happen. Why should he? He's got it made the way his is—women on tap whenever he wants them, and no strings to tie him down.'

'You don't think perhaps Barbara Lange is different?' Alysha forced herself to enquire; Gemma knew him as well as anyone—her opinion ought to be valid.

Gemma conceded a wry smile. 'Maybe,' she mused. 'But I doubt if it'll stop him having a bit on the side, if the opportunity presents itself. The man's a selfish, arrogant, egotistical louse, and I pity any poor girl who's stupid enough to fall in love with him.'

The acid that had crept into her tone belied her pretence of indifference—Alysha couldn't help feeling a little sorry for her. But it made her more than ever determined to keep her own wayward emotions under strict control.

'Well, I have no intention whatsoever of falling in love with him—nor of going to bed with him,' she asserted, trying to feign a profound interest in her book. 'I admit he's...extremely attractive—if you like

that type. But our relationship is purely
professional . . .'

Gemma sniggered. 'That's what they all say—and
the next thing you know their knickers are on the
bedpost. Anyway, I've got a fiver on it for Thursday—
and I've got a feeling I'm not going to lose my money.'
And with a lazy stretch she rose to her feet and strolled
over to the pool, sitting down on the edge to flirt with
some of the men from the television crew.

Alysha lay back on her sun-lounger, trying to concentrate on her book, but the words were jumbled on
the page. Vivid images—of Ross snapping his fingers,
of her own dainty white lace briefs hanging on the
post of a big double-size hotel bed—were swirling in
her mind; images of that powerful male body crushing
hers, his hard hands caressing her tender breasts, his
rough thighs parting hers to thrust between, right into
the deepest core of her . . .

'Still not swimming? Afraid to get your swimsuit
wet?'

At the sound of that sardonic voice, her heart
kicked against her ribs, and she was mortifyingly
aware of the deep rush of colour that flooded her
cheeks. 'I . . . Yes, maybe I might now,' she managed,
her voice unsteady. Maybe the chill of that clear,
sparkling water might cool the fevered heat in her
blood.

She rose quickly, and slipped off her shirt, far too
conscious of those assessing grey eyes sliding down
over the length of her slender body in the caressing
Lycra hug of her swimsuit, lingering over every curve.
Her breasts seemed almost to swell beneath that intimate gaze, achingly ripe, the nipples hardening to

taut buds that she knew must be clearly visible beneath the clinging fabric.

'Don't stay in for too long, though,' he warned, a lilt of lazy mockery in his tone. 'We don't want any strap-marks on that delicate skin.' He put out one hand, and with the tip of his finger traced a path that followed the neckline of her swimsuit, from her shoulder down into the soft hint of shadow between her breasts. 'It would be a pity to damage something so...perfect.'

Alysha felt trapped, helpless in the mesmerising spell he was weaving around her. 'He has whoever he wants...' A knowing smile curved the corners of that disturbingly sensuous mouth. 'All he has to do is snap his fingers...'

It took every ounce of will-power she possessed to turn away from him. The cool water swallowed her up as she dived gracefully in, and she swam across the bottom right to the other side, only surfacing when she touched the far wall.

She had half expected Ross to follow her, but he hadn't. Tipping back her head, she dipped it into the water to smooth her hair back from her face, the sun bright against her closed eyelids. She hoped none of the others would come over and speak to her—she didn't feel as though she could face any of them just yet.

Anger and humiliation were warring inside her; anger at knowing that they were all taking bets with each other on how quickly Ross could succeed in persuading her to sleep with him—and humiliation because she had an uncomfortable feeling that one of them was going to collect the jackpot.

When at last she turned, it was to see Ross on the far side of the pool, romping with Gemma—she was sitting on his shoulders, shrieking with laughter as Doug and some of the others tried to dislodge her.

A stab of pure jealousy, so sharp it almost took her breath away, struck her heart. Gemma was right—he was a selfish, egotistical louse who wouldn't hesitate to enjoy a bit on the side with any woman who was willing. And Gemma was making it abundantly clear that she was willing.

Did Barbara know what he got up to behind her back? Alysha wondered angrily. She probably did— she was no fool. But maybe she didn't mind—maybe she was wise enough and secure enough to allow him a long leash, knowing that her own attractions would ultimately bring him back to her, no matter how frequently he might roam.

'Oh, my lord—will you just take a look out here! I think I've died and gone to Paradise!'

Alysha, stepping down from the camper-van behind Alastair, could only agree with his breathless remark as she gazed around in wonder at the scene emerging from the early morning mist. This was what they had risen before dawn, and driven for more than three hours over poor roads and rutted tracks, to find.

They were in a small clearing, in the heart of the dense tropical rainforest. All around the chatter of birds and the screech of monkeys filled the warm, still air, against a lilting counterpoint of water splashing over a waterfall somewhere a short distance away.

'Perfect,' Ross approved. 'What do you think, Harry?'

The photographer nodded. 'Yes. But we'll have to get to work pretty soon—it's already coming on for seven-thirty.'

Ross nodded. 'How long will it take you to get her ready, Alastair?'

The older man pursed his lips, indignant at being rushed. 'Well, I really don't know. It depends if you want a slapdash job—that I can do in ten minutes. But if you want it done properly...'

'Can you be finished for half-eight?'

'If you say so.'

Ross smiled with that easy charm that would always win him co-operation. 'Try? That will give us an hour to scout for exactly where we're going to shoot, and get the equipment set up. Harry, what do you have in mind here?' he added, moving away.

Alysha refused to let herself betray the least flicker of resentment that he hadn't bothered to address so much as a single word to her—she was just the model, after all. Her job was simply to wear what she was told and stand where she was told—it wasn't necessary to treat her like a human being.

It hadn't been like that yesterday, though. Why the difference? Was it because yesterday he had been trying to lure her into his bed—whereas now he had no need to bother, having someone else to warm it for him?

Of course, she might be jumping to conclusions, she conceded grimly; after all, he might have taken Gemma out to dinner last night simply to talk about work—and it might have been no more than coincidence that they had come downstairs together this morning. And that smug look on Gemma's face could have been caused by almost anything.

Yes, and pigs might fly. Well, so much for the crew's sweepstake, anyway—they would have to abandon it now. That was some compensation, at least—the thought of them all sniggering as they waited for her to succumb to Ross Elliot's practised seduction technique had been unbearable.

Alastair didn't like early mornings, and he was in a petulant mood, grumbling under his breath all the time he was working on her face—much to the delight of the documentary crew, who had been becoming a little bored with the lack of conflict on the shoot. Nevertheless he worked deftly, brushing and blending, transforming her face into the flawless work of art the cameras would capture. By twenty past eight, wearing another sarong—blue and green this time— and another wide-brimmed straw hat, she was ready.

Ross and Harry, and the TV commercial crew, were deep in discussion, checking light-meters and testing camera angles. As Alysha approached, shepherded by Gemma with a tangle of different necklaces over her arm and Alastair with his box of cosmetic tricks, Ross glanced around.

'Hmm.' That coolly critical gaze swept down over her, registering not so much as a flicker of personal interest. 'I'm not sure about the way you've got that top wrapped, Gemma—it's covering up too much. Can you make it a little briefer?'

'Of course. Here, can you hold these for a minute, Alysha?'

Alysha took the hank of necklaces while the stylist adjusted the narrow strip of fabric that covered her breasts.

'Better?' she enquired.

Ross nodded brisk approval of the effect Gemma had achieved. 'That'll do. I like the colours in that thing, Gem—they'll really stand out against the background here.'

The other girl preened with pleasure at such praise. 'I've brought a few necklaces for her to wear—what do you think?' she enquired eagerly.

'No jewellery,' he insisted, shaking his head. 'It would clutter up the look—we want to show off her skin, not what she's wearing.'

Alysha flashed him a look of cold fury; he was still talking about her as if she couldn't even hear him. Just for a second something glinted in those mocking grey eyes, something that made her heartbeat skid and start to race. But then he had turned away, strolling up the path towards where the camper-van was now parked.

'OK, let's get started. Are you all set, Harry?'

With an effort of will, Alysha forced the lid back on to the cauldron of emotions that was boiling inside her. What was there to get excited about, after all? Apparently she was only his *third* choice, after Bobbie and Gemma! If that wasn't enough to make her realise what a fool she was being, what would?

After all, what was so special about him anyway? Studied objectively, he wasn't even particularly good-looking. A pair of eyes the colour of a Glaswegian winter sky, a mouth that could be both cruel and sensual, a long, lean, hard-muscled body...

No—she had to stop thinking about him. If it were only Gemma she had to compete with, she might have felt some confidence; but there was Bobbie too—and quite apart from the fact that she was a friend, she knew she couldn't match that indefinable aura of sophistication and worldly wisdom the older woman exuded so effortlessly.

Forcing her mind back to the job in hand, she followed the others up the path that led through the tangled jungle. They were gathered in a small knot, and as she approached she realised that the path continued on to a narrow rope and plank bridge that spanned a deep ravine, with a river at the bottom. She hesitated, an uncomfortable sense of foreboding filling her.

'I...hope you're not going to ask me to walk across that thing?' she enquired a little unsteadily.

Ross glanced around at her, one dark eyebrow lifted in sardonic enquiry. 'It's perfectly safe—we've been across it ourselves. Not afraid of heights, are you?'

'No,' she countered, her eyes sparking. 'But I *am* afraid of crocodiles. And don't try telling me there aren't any, because I'm quite sure there are.'

Ross lifted his wide shoulders in a dismissive shrug. 'I dare say you're right. But there's no reason why you should fall in, so there's no need for you to worry about them.'

'It's going to be the most fabulous shot,' Gemma enthused. 'I've never seen such a glorious setting.'

Alysha was forced to agree. Below them the river was like a mirror, perfectly reflecting the overhanging trees in its tranquil brown surface. But that bridge looked terrifyingly flimsy. It was no use telling herself that the local people probably used it a dozen times a day—she didn't like the look of it.

'OK, go out to the middle, and walk back towards us,' Ross instructed briskly. 'Don't rush it—the mood is languid, easy.'

Alysha slanted him a glittering glare from beneath her lashes, but chose not to give him the satisfaction of an argument. Drawing in a deep, steadying breath, she stepped out cautiously on to the bridge, trying not to look down through the gaps between the planks at the dark water twenty feet below.

Actually, it wasn't so bad. The planks were a little slippery with the green lichen that thrived in the warm, moist atmosphere, and the slight swaying was decidedly alarming, but if she trod carefully she would be all right. She made her way out to the centre, and turned.

'All right?'

'Back a little more.'

She obeyed. 'Here?'

'That's fine. Now, walk this way. Keep your head up—you don't need to watch your feet.'

Anyone who thought modelling was a picnic would have had to admit, after watching the shoot that morning, that they were wrong. As the sun climbed into the high blue sky, the air beneath the canopy of trees became like a sauna, laden with humid heat that soon had everyone without a specific job to do retreating into the comparative cool of the camper-van.

Alysha was beginning to suspect that Ross must have a sadistic streak. He was leaning against a convenient tree-trunk, his arms folded across his wide chest, watching her calmly as she picked her way precariously along the bridge, trying to look languid while the director of the television commercial made her repeat the simple line of dialogue over and over.

'Lozier have taken natural ingredients from the forest . . .'

Disaster struck with no warning at all. One moment the sun was blazing down, the next it was raining— great heavy drops falling out of the sky and sizzling as they hit the hot wooden bridge. Behind her there was a screech, and a flock of bright birds swooped up out of the trees. Startled, she turned—and her foot slipped, knocking one of the planks and sending it spinning down into the water below.

She screamed, grabbing at the rope hand-rail as she fell.

For one terrifying moment she swung over the yawning gap; and then Ross was there, catching her around the waist and scooping her to safety. She clung to him, shaking violently, as the drenching rain stung her skin. The straw hat she had been wearing had fallen into the water, but it didn't float there for long— from beneath the dark surface a sinister shape emerged, and two powerful jaws snapped clean through it.

'All right—you're all right,' Ross soothed, holding her close as she shuddered in horror. 'I've got you— I won't let you fall.'

His mouth came down on hers in a sizzling kiss that was almost savage in its intensity, his tongue swirling deep into her mouth, flagrantly sensual, claiming right of possession over every sweet, sensitive corner within. And she responded just as fiercely, her blood heated with a fever that made her head swim.

But even as her physical responses skidded wildly out of control, the cauldron of her emotions finally boiled over, and she recoiled from him, shock turning to blazing anger. 'You said it was safe!' she flashed, her voice raised above the crackle and hiss of the falling rain, turning to steam around them as it hit the sun-baked wooden planks of the bridge. 'If I *had* fallen in, it would have been all your fault.'

'Alysha . . .'

'Leave me alone! Don't touch me,' she spat, stepping back swiftly as he reached for her—even the slippery rain-soaked bridge seemed preferable to his treacherous embrace.

'I was just going to help you back to the bank,' he offered gently.

'I can manage by myself, thank you.'

He shrugged his wide shoulders, his mouth compressed with taut impatience, but stood aside to let her pass.

She squinted through the sheets of rain; it seemed a horribly long way to the safety of the bank. For a moment she regretted her hasty dismissal of his assistance—but she certainly wasn't going to give him the satisfaction of changing her mind. She could do it by herself.

It seemed to take for ever. Hanging on grimly to the guard-rope, she worked her way hand-over-hand along the bridge; her hair was plastered to her head, the wet sarong almost transparent against her long, slender legs. But though she was aware of him following close behind her, a protective shadow, she steadfastly ignored him.

At last she made it; the rest of the crew reached out to haul her the last few steps to safety, hustling her into the shelter of the camper-van.

'Lord, you look like a drowned rat!' Alastair protested, hurrying forward with a towel. 'Sit down and let me dry your hair, or it will be all over the place.

And just look at those bruises...! It's going to be horrendous trying to cover those up.'

'Sorry to have damaged the merchandise,' Ross remarked sardonically as he followed her into the van. Ignoring her fulminating glare, he bent and lifted her foot to examine her injured ankle; she had scraped it on the plank as she had fallen, and only now did she realise how much it hurt. 'There's a few splinters in there that had better come out. Get me the first-aid box, someone.'

Gemma brought it, and Ross took out a pair of tweezers, squatting on the floor and propping her bare foot in his lap.

'This may hurt,' he warned grimly.

It did, though contrary to her expectations his touch was incredibly gentle as he tackled the splinters one by one. She winced in pain, tears stinging her eyes; she tried to blink them back, but their cause was more complex than the superficial physical hurt. And at least that gave her a real excuse to cry; in fact it was almost a relief to let the tears fall.

At last the job was finished. Ross bathed the whole area, and dabbed on a little antiseptic. 'There—that ought to be all right now,' he remarked, straightening. 'I think you'll live.'

'Thank you.' She managed a crooked smile, reluctantly abandoning her anger with him. 'And...thank you for coming out on to the bridge for me,' she added a little awkwardly.

He acknowledged her words with a flicker of sardonic amusement. 'Think nothing of it. It would have been a shame to have wasted all the footage we've shot so far by having to start again with another model.'

There was laughter from the rest of the crew. 'I warned you—he's a slave-driver!' Alastair declared with mock indignation. 'Well, you're going to *have* to give her a day off now—that ankle's going to be a mess, and even I'm not going to be able to disguise it.'

CHAPTER SIX

'HELLO, sweetie.' Alastair flopped languidly into a spare seat at the table—it was happy hour at the terrace bar, which with typical Thai hospitality was actually two hours long, with all the drinks at half price. 'How's the ankle doing?'

'Not too badly, thank you,' Alysha responded with a smile. 'The swelling's almost gone down now, and there's only a little bit of bruising.'

'They should never have made you go out on that bridge,' Alastair insisted with a theatrical shudder. 'It never looked safe to me. I hope you're going to put in a massive claim for damages!'

'Ross has already contacted the insurance people about it,' Alysha confirmed wryly.

'Hmph!' Alastair pursed his lips. 'Well, don't let them fob you off with a measly settlement. You could have been killed!'

'Yes, well . . . I prefer not to think too much about it,' she responded, a note of constraint in her voice; it wasn't so much the incident itself that disturbed her as the memory of being caught up in Ross's strong, protective arms, of his gentleness as he had taken the splinters out . . .

The sound of loud laughter cut across the exotic tropical gardens in which the bar was set. Alastair lifted his sunglasses, peering around. 'Is that our Gemma, or one of those damned parakeets?' he enquired with wicked raillery—the gardens also housed an aviary of tropical birds, including a dozen parakeets and macaws that were allowed to fly free and were inclined to startle unwary guests by landing on their tables and demanding titbits.

'I think it's Gemma,' Alysha confirmed. The other girl was coming towards them, laden with shopping-bags, Doug at her side.

Alastair chuckled. 'Well, well—looks as if she's decided to settle for what she can get,' he surmised. 'Sensible girl. She was always riding for a fall, trying to set her cap at Ross again.'

Alysha slanted him a look of surprise. 'Oh? I'd...rather got the impression...there was something going on between them again.'

Alastair shrugged eloquently. 'It's possible,' he conceded. 'Though I'm afraid it wouldn't have been anything more a one-night stand. Too available, you see. Let me give you a little word of advice there,' he added, leaning towards her and speaking in a conspiratorial murmur. 'With a man like that, you must always keep him wanting just that little bit more than you're giving. That way he'll stay hungry.'

Alysha almost choked. 'I...don't know what you mean,' she protested, knowing she wasn't making a very good job of deceiving him. 'Why should I want him to stay hungry? We're not... There isn't any... He's still seeing Barbara Lange, so far as I know.'

He lifted one neatly arched eyebrow, slanting her a look that implied he could say a great deal more if he chose, but at that moment Gemma and Doug joined them, Gemma dumping her shopping on one chair and collapsing into another.

'Phew—I'm bushed!' she declared inelegantly, raising an imperious hand to summon a waiter. 'Get me a Golden Sunset,' she demanded, ordering the delicious cocktail of kahlua and mango juice that had become everyone's favourite at the end of a hot, tiring day.

Alastair cast a jaded eye over the mountain of bags she had brought in. 'It looks as if you've been in training for the Olympic shop-till-you-drop competition,' he remarked drily.

Gemma laughed. 'I think I have!' she conceded merrily. 'We've been down to the market on Ratchparop Road—you can get fake Gucci T-shirts there for less than a pound each...'

Alysha wasn't really listening; her mind was puzzling over that strange conversation with Alastair. He had the reputation for always being several jumps ahead of everyone else when it came to knowing what was going on. Well, she wouldn't be surprised if he was right about Gemma, she mused, watching the other girl covertly from beneath her lashes; she was sparkling just a little too brightly today—had she already been used and discarded? If so, she couldn't help feeling a little sorry for her; she should have known better, of course, but she knew only too well herself that bitter experience was no protection where Ross Elliot was concerned.

But what had he been implying about Barbara? Did he really know something that no one else did...?

'Well, I suppose I'd better go and get my packing done,' Gemma announced, swinging herself to her feet. 'The bus leaves for the airport at half six.'

Alysha glanced up at her sharply. 'Half past six tonight?' she queried, bewildered. 'But... I didn't think we were going until tomorrow?'

'*You* are,' the other girl responded airily. 'I'm off home.'

'You aren't coming to Ko Samui?'

Gemma shook her head, shrugging her slim, sun-tanned shoulders. 'They don't need me there—they're only doing the nude shots.'

Alysha felt the blood drain from her cheeks, and then flood back in a wave of scarlet. 'N-nude shots?'

'Yes.' Gemma regarded her in condescending amusement. 'Didn't you know?'

'No... No, I didn't...' There was a strange ringing sound in her ears. She put down her glass and rose to her feet, every movement very slow, very controlled. 'Excuse me, I... The sun's giving me a bit of a headache,' she stammered, all her usual ability to hide her emotions deserting her. 'I think I'll... go inside for a little while.'

She held herself very erect as she walked away. She knew that her pathetic excuse had fooled no one— they were probably all laughing at her behind her back right now. But somehow she managed to get herself out of the bar. A small nuclear explosion was going off inside her head—when she found Ross, she would *kill* him!

The moment came sooner than she had expected; by chance he was coming out of the lift as she reached it, with Harry Keaton. She barely even saw the photographer, confronting Ross with her eyes blazing, her jaw taut. 'If you have a moment,' she ground out, 'I'd like a few words with you—in private.'

He lifted one dark eyebrow in mild astonishment. 'Certainly,' he conceded. 'Shall we go upstairs? Excuse me, Harry—I'll be with you in a little while.'

He stepped back into the lift, and Alysha followed him automatically. He slanted her a speculative glance, but neither of them spoke as they rode up to his floor, nor as she walked beside him down the corridor. He opened the door to his suite and gestured politely for her to step inside.

For a moment then she hesitated; maybe it would have been better to stay downstairs, after all. But there was nowhere down there where they could talk in private—and besides, in her present frame of mind, if he so much as laid a finger on her she would cripple him for life. So she swept regally past him, all her hackles bristling.

He followed her into the room, closing the door behind him.

The suite was large—much larger than hers—with a spectacular view over the Chao Phraya river to the gracefully towering chedi of the Temple of the Dawn on the far bank. She walked across to the window, her jaw tense with agitation, gazing out at the panoramic vista with unseeing eyes.

'So, what did you want to talk about?' he prompted, a faintly mocking inflection in his voice.

She had been trying to rehearse a speech, a few well-chosen, cutting words that would leave him floundering, but at his question her mind went completely blank. 'I . . . er . . . It was about the trip to Ko Samui,' she managed, her voice unsteady. 'I was wondering . . . which outfits you were intending me to wear?'

'I wasn't,' he responded evenly. 'You won't be wearing anything.'

She turned to stare at him in shock—she hadn't expected him to admit it quite so blatantly. 'You mean it's true?' she demanded. 'I didn't believe it when Gemma told me . . .!'

His expression was one of strained tolerance. 'We're advertising skin-care—so we're showing skin. What did you expect to be wearing—a fur coat and leather thigh-boots?'

'I've been wearing something up to now,' she threw back at him with haughty disdain. 'Not a lot, it's true, but at least I was decent.'

'The beach shots are for stage two of the campaign,' he spelled out with cool precision. 'No television, just stills for the magazines.'

'I don't work nude,' she asserted. 'It's in my contract.'

'Where?'

She stared at him aghast. 'It's always in. Bobbie knows . . . She always makes sure it's in . . .'

He shook his head. 'Not this time. Check it if you like.'

He walked over to the desk, and opened his briefcase, drawing out a red plastic folder. As he handed it to her, she recognised the contract Barbara had given her to sign. Frantically she flicked through it—she hadn't bothered at the time, trusting Barbara as her agent to ensure that it was all in order.

'As you can see, there's no such clause.'

Her eyes were blazing in fury as she glared up at him. 'You must have taken it out!' she accused. 'You tricked me . . .!'

'Not at all,' he countered coolly. 'I made it quite clear to Bobbie that I would specifically require you to do nude shots. No doubt she assumed, as I did, that on this occasion you would have no objection.'

Alysha felt the ground shifting beneath her. She was appalled that Bobbie could have betrayed her like this—but then Bobbie was first and foremost a businesswoman. She wanted the prestige this contract would bring—and she would have been quite prepared to override a few scruples to get it.

But though he might have her cornered, she wasn't going to give in without a fight. She tilted up her chin, regarding him in haughty disdain. 'Well, I do object,' she informed him forcefully. 'I won't do it.'

'Then I shall sue you for breaking your contract,' he responded, a measure of quiet menace in his voice. 'I've put a great deal of time and work into this campaign, and I'm not going to allow you to wreck it now because of some contrary little whim. And believe me, I don't make idle threats. You may be able to afford the cost financially, but you'll kiss goodbye to your precious career—for good. Pretty models are ten a penny, and no one's going to hire a girl with a name for being difficult.'

'I'm not being difficult.' She was having to fight to hold back the tide of panic that was rising inside her. She could have no doubt that he really would take her to court—and she couldn't afford to lose; she would be hard pressed even to afford a lawyer to defend the case for her. But she wasn't going to let him know that. 'I'm entitled to maintain my professional reputation—everyone knows I never work nude.'

'Never?' He turned back to his briefcase and took out another folder, which he tossed down on the desk. 'What do you call those?'

She stared at the envelope, knowing exactly what was in it. Her knees were wobbling alarmingly, and she sat down heavily. The folder had fallen open as he had tossed it down, and the contents were spilling out—a batch of glossy eight-by-ten black and white prints, beautifully reproduced, every detail clear.

She saw her own youthful face, smiling uncertainly into the camera—the expression was not unlike that of a scared rabbit, trapped in the beam of a car's headlights. Her bare shoulders, too, betrayed her tension; her professional eye frowned at such pathetic amateurism—had she really been so gauche?

The lighting of the pictures was superb, capturing the soft, peach-like texture of the skin over those firm, naked breasts, the fine, delicate pucker of her taut nipples. She could appreciate the technical expertise, even as she felt an icy chill run through her. He had remembered all along.

Her hands were trembling as she stared at the photographs. Their existence had always haunted her; she had dreaded that he might one day publish them, as he was perfectly entitled to do—she had signed the model release. And now he was using them to force her to do as he wished. Those pictures as evidence would undermine any legal defence she might have.

Ross glanced down at her, and then crossed swiftly to the drinks cabinet on the far side of the room, returning with a stiff measure of brandy. She took it from him automatically; but then some lingering spirit of defiance reasserted itself, and she shook her head, trying to give it back to him.

'I don't want it.'

'Drink it,' he ordered. 'You look as though you need it.'

To her humiliation she didn't seem to have the strength of will to resist him, even in such a small matter—and in spite of the fact that she didn't much care for brandy. She drank it quickly, wrinkling up her nose in disgust.

'That's good,' he approved, taking the glass from her and putting it back, and then sitting down casually in one of the deep, comfortable armchairs that furnished the suite. 'Now, let's discuss this shoot.'

She slanted him a glittering look from beneath her lashes. 'What is there to discuss?' she demanded bitterly. 'I don't have any option, do I?'

'No,' he acknowledged with a grim smile. 'However, I think you're worrying unnecessarily. I've no more wish to be associated with a campaign that relies on gratuitous titillation than you have. Besides, we're aiming at a female market, and all the research suggests that that sort of approach wouldn't get the sort of response we want.'

She shook her head. 'I don't care how tastefully you try to dress it up,' she retorted. 'I'm still going to have to pose naked in front of the cameras, aren't I?'

'Yes—but not full-frontal. In fact, most of the shots will be from behind. Or else composed in such a way that nothing . . . important is showing. There's going to be nothing you could be embarrassed about.'

'But . . . the crew will be there—I'll have to take my clothes off in front of them . . .' Her voice fractured; tears welled into her eyes, but she struggled to blink them back, not wanting him to think she was using them as a weapon to gain his sympathy. 'I can't do it—I can't.'

'Is that what's bothering you the most?' he asked; the unexpectedly gentle tone of his voice was treacherously disarming—or was it the effect of the brandy? 'Undressing in front of the crew?'

She nodded dumbly.

'All right—what if it were just me?'

She stared at him in blank confusion. 'You?'

He nodded. 'What if I took the pictures? I'm sure we'd be able to manage well enough without the rest of the crew—they're all beach shots, so the lighting isn't going to be a problem, and most of the angles aren't going to require make-up anyway.'

'But...don't you have to get back to England?' she argued unsteadily.

'There's nothing that can't wait a few more days,' he responded with a casual shrug of his wide shoulders. 'Christmas is coming—no one's going to be doing much work anyway. And I'm quite sure the crew won't object to an early release—they'll still get paid.'

Alysha could feel herself trembling. All the memories of that long-ago afternoon in his studio were flooding back into her mind, and the muscles of her stomach were knotting just as they had when she had stood there in front of him in that low-slung sarong, her breasts naked...

But the alternative was even more unthinkable— Harry might not be too bad, but Doug... She could just imagine him, leering at her...

'A-all right,' she conceded, her throat constricted. 'If I...have to do it, I'd...rather it was you.'

He nodded, accepting her capitulation with no show of triumph. 'I'll let the others know there's been a change of plan,' he said quietly. 'Are you coming down to dinner?'

She shook her head, rising unsteadily to her feet. 'No, I...don't think so,' she demurred weakly. 'I'm...not very hungry. I think I'll...just go straight to my room.'

He took her hand, his fingers strong around hers. 'Get some sleep,' he advised, a note of concern in his voice that she could almost believe was really for her, not just for the way she would look in front of the camera tomorrow if she had bags beneath her eyes. 'Our flight isn't until eleven, but we'd better leave for the airport at about half nine to allow for the traffic.'

She nodded, unable to make herself quite meet his eyes. 'All right. I'll...see you in the morning, then. Goodnight.'

'Goodnight.' He let her go, and she escaped swiftly from the luxurious suite. As the door closed behind her she drew in a long, ragged breath. What on earth had she let herself in for? Three days alone with him, on some deserted beach, and at her most vulnerable...

But he had made it quite clear that he intended to get the photographs he wanted—and he was absolutely ruthless enough to carry out his threat to take her to court. And if those pictures he had taken before were made public... She shuddered in horror at the mere thought. The tabloid Press would have a field day with them!

No, she didn't have any choice. She was just going to have to make it very clear to him that they would be there to work—and nothing else. That shouldn't be too difficult, she tried hard to reassure herself; five years ago she had been a lamb to the slaughter—it wouldn't be like that this time.

* * *

The island was a tropical paradise, a tiny emerald jewel set in a sparkling turquoise sea. They had flown down to the tiny airport on Ko Samui, an island in the Gulf of Thailand, and from there they had picked up a small but extremely luxurious motor yacht—thirty-two feet of gleaming white hull, with a spacious, air-conditioned cabin upholstered in cool blue and white, and state-of-the-art satellite navigation.

It had taken them a little less than an hour to reach this place, but it could have been a thousand miles from anywhere, a tiny dot lost between the horizon of sky and sea. Steep cliffs of ragged yellow lime-stone, tangled with a dense jungle of mangroves and casuarinas, plunged straight into the sea, except for just one spot where they overhung a sheltered cove, with a beach of soft white coral sand lapped by the crystal waters of a shallow lagoon.

Ross ran the yacht in close, and dropped the anchor. Peering over the side, Alysha could see schools of bright fish darting between the rocks and small clusters of coral on the sandy bottom. It looked only inches deep, but she guessed that it must be more like five or six feet.

'What do you think?'

Paradise. A soft, warm breeze fanned a strand of her dark, silken hair across her cheek, and she brushed it back. 'It's...very nice,' she managed, her voice stiff with the effort of keeping her churning emotions under control.

They had spoken little since they had shared a breakfast-table at the hotel back in Bangkok early this morning; his manner towards her had been as pro-fessional as she could wish, but she couldn't relax, not with the prospect ahead of her of three days alone with him on this small boat—three days and two nights.

'We can't start work for a couple of hours yet,' he remarked, glancing up at the angle of the sun. 'I think I'll take a swim. There could be some interesting fish along that coral reef.' He slanted her a questioning glance. 'Want to join me?'

'No, thank you,' she responded tautly. 'I'd rather get on with my book.'

He glanced down at the thick paperback she was reading. '*The Alexandria Quartet*? A bit heavy going for this weather, isn't it?' he remarked, a sardonic inflection in his voice.

She shrugged her slender shoulders, resolutely maintaining the air of haughty superiority that was her only defence against him. 'I prefer real literature to the kind of sex-and-shopping pap that passes for a novel these days,' she returned, aware that she sounded like the most appalling snob.

Something dark and faintly menacing flickered behind those steel-grey eyes, but then with an amiable grin he kicked off his sandals. 'Everyone to their own taste,' he conceded equably. He grasped the bottom of his T-shirt, and with one lithe, easy movement peeled it off over his head. 'Would you rub some suncream on my back?'

She caught her breath so sharply she almost choked.

'Might as well find out if this stuff does the job it's supposed to do,' he pointed out, that hard mouth curved into a smile of lazy mockery as he held out the tube of cream to her.

She rose unsteadily to her feet, her heart pounding so hard she was afraid he would be able to hear it. But what reason could she give for refusing? He would

know it was just an excuse—and he would laugh at
her cowardice. Her hands were shaking slightly as she
took the tube from him, and unscrewed the cap.

His dominating height overshadowed her, and there
was something almost . . . feral about that thick pelt
of rough, dark hair that curled across his wide chest—
it was all she could do to fight back the impulse to
run her fingertips through it.

'T-turn round, then,' she stammered thickly.

Only by the faint flicker of sardonic humour that
lifted the corners of that disturbingly attractive mouth
did he reveal that he was aware of the effort it was
costing her to maintain that cool façade. Hooking his
thumbs casually into the waistband of his low-slung
shorts, he turned his back to her.

It was no better. She hesitated for a moment, reluctant to take the risk of actually touching him—
afraid that she wouldn't be able to control the heated
desire that was smouldering inside her. But with an
effort of will she at last managed to pull herself
together enough to pour a little of the sun-cream into
her hand.

His skin was warm and smooth under her palm,
the muscle and bone beneath as hard as rock. Slicking
the cream across his wide shoulders, she began to
massage it in, slowly, circling over his broad back and
down the deep cleft of his spine. She wanted him—
wanted him with a fierce, aching hunger that was
eating her up inside. She wanted to wrap her arms
around him, feel the hard length of his body against
hers . . .

'Thank you—I think that ought to be enough
for now.'

The inflection of mocking amusement in his voice brought Alysha abruptly to her senses, and she realised that she had taken far longer over the task than had been strictly necessary. She stepped back quickly, fumbling to put the top back on the tube of cream.

'I'll see you later, then,' he said, slanting her a smile that could have meant whatever she wanted it to mean.

She nodded, not trusting herself to speak. It was just as well he was taking himself off for a while, she reflected with a small tremor of agitation—she needed a little time alone to calm herself down.

But that didn't prove easy. Maybe it was the heat; even with the soft sea-breeze drifting across the water, she was aware of a fine sheen of sweat across her brow. She was trying to read, but it was impossible to concentrate; her mind had no defence against the disturbing images that were flooding into it.

At last she gave up any pretence of resistance, letting her book fall on to her lap and closing her eyes, surrendering to the sweet temptation of those dangerous fantasies. She could almost feel his hands caressing her naked breasts, sliding over her slim, silken thighs... A soft moan escaped her lips, and she moved her body with unconscious sensuality as the boat swayed gently on the shallow water.

She knew that she was only fuelling the fires, but the need was too powerful to control; and it would probably be only a very short time now before the images would become a physical reality. Wasn't that the real reason he had suggested they should come here together, the real reason she had agreed?

And the most humiliating thing was that she knew how little it meant to him—she was no more than a minor diversion, and when it was over he would go back to Barbara as if nothing had happened. Which was worse—betraying her friend, or betraying her own self-respect?

But even though she was disgusted to have to admit that she could sink so low, she didn't know how to escape her fate. She had been branded by him the first time he had kissed her, and though it had taken him five years to claim his prerogative it had been inevitable from that moment. She belonged to him, and whenever he chose to take her she could only surrender.

Languid sleep seeped into her brain, a sleep filled with strange, fevered dreams...

She woke with a start to the sting of ice against her bare midriff. Ross was grinning down at her, trailing an ice-cube across a narrow gap that had opened between her loose T-shirt and her shorts. She sat up quickly, stabbing him a look of hot indignation.

'Had a good sleep?' Ross enquired, a provocative glint in his eyes as he popped the ice-cube into his mouth and sucked on it—a very deliberate invocation of their first meeting, five years ago.

'Yes, thank you,' Alysha responded, struggling to regain the air of aloof disdain she had been cultivating all morning—though she couldn't quite look him in the eye, afraid he would see some shadow of those lingering dreams in them.

'Coke?'

'Thank you.' She took the can he was holding out to her, sipping it gratefully—it was now a little after three-thirty, and the steaming heat of the tropical afternoon lay heavily all around them.

He sat down on the opposite seat, leaning back and draining his can in one long draught. 'I had a look round the far side of the island,' he remarked lazily. 'It's rockier than this side, but there are one or two spots there worth investigating. The light will be good enough to start work in a little while. I thought we'd start on the beach—there beneath that overhang where the creepers are trailing down.'

'OK.' She made herself draw in a long, steadying breath, keeping her voice very controlled. 'What do you want me to do?'

'I thought we could have you sitting in the sand, right at the water's edge, with your back to the camera—it should frame nicely in the arch formed by the rocks and the creepers, and the sun will be at just the right angle.'

'OK.'

'No arguments?' he taunted, a provocative glint in those steel-grey eyes.

'No.'

He laughed in lazy mockery. 'That makes a change.'

She returned him a look of icy disdain. 'Since you've blackmailed me into posing naked for you, there's not a great deal I can argue about, is there?' she retorted.

He lifted one dark eyebrow in sardonic amusement. 'Blackmail? That's a very strong word,' he argued, unruffled. 'I was simply insisting that you kept to your contract.'

'Why was it so essential anyway?' she bit out, acid on her tongue. 'Why couldn't I have worn a bikini or something?'

'Because I wanted you naked,' he returned with uncompromising insistence. 'That's why I hired you.'

'For the campaign, or for your own benefit?' she challenged recklessly.

He chuckled in wicked amusement. 'What do you think?'

She glared back at him, her eyes sparking with fury. 'I think you planned it this way. I think you chose this place because you...want to...'

He completed her sentence with a word so explicit that it made her choke. 'You knew that,' he asserted ruthlessly. 'And what's more, you want it as much as I do. Don't even try to deny it—your body-language gives you away.'

A flood of heat coloured her cheeks with pink as she realised that it was true; beneath his mocking gaze her breasts were aching and full, the tender nipples ripened to hard buds that were clearly outlined beneath the soft cotton of her T-shirt.

He had caught her eyes, holding them with that compelling gaze. 'I want you,' he reiterated, his voice taking on a husky timbre. 'I've wanted you from the very first moment I saw you.'

She stared at him in shock. 'But...I was only seventeen then,' she protested raggedly.

'I know,' he conceded with a soft laugh. 'Despicable of me, wasn't it? I don't expect you to believe me, but I really had no intention of touching you that day—merely to teach you a sorely needed lesson. You thought your money could buy you anything—including me. So I decided to show you that modelling isn't just an amusing little game for a bored little rich girl to play at. But you know, even though I gave you a really hard time, you did pretty well,' he added reflectively. 'I was impressed.'

Alysha was surprised by his words, but she wasn't going to risk lowering her defences by so much as an inch. 'Oh?' she returned in glacial accents. 'And I suppose you were just teaching me a lesson when you got me to pose...topless for you.'

'Partly. You were taking a very foolish risk, you know, going straight to a photographer without the protection of an agency referral—you could have found yourself in much deeper water than you did with me.'

She lifted one delicately arched eyebrow in frank scepticism. 'It seemed quite deep enough,' she countered caustically.

'Yes, well... Unfortunately, things...got a little out of control.' That fascinating mouth curved into a smile of lazy reminiscence. 'And you ran off like Cinderella at the stroke of midnight, before I could apologise—leaving me with just a batch of photographs, instead of a glass slipper. Though I must admit,' he added, his eyes glinting with wicked humour, 'they were a lot more interesting to look at.'

A wave of heat swept over her at the memory of those shameful pictures. 'You...could have apologised when we met again,' she pointed out stiffly.

'True,' he conceded, a lilt of mocking humour in his voice. 'But I took one look at you all grown up, and I knew I wasn't a bit sorry—on the contrary, I was rather looking forward to exploring the possibilities further.'

'And is that why you gave me the contract?' she demanded. 'Because you thought I'd let you...' She felt her cheeks flame scarlet again at the memory of the crude word he had used—there was no way she could repeat it.

He laughed, shaking his head. 'Of course not. Oh, I've been watching your progress with considerable interest, I won't deny that—it was quite gratifying to see the talent I'd first spotted developing as you gained in experience. And I was hearing very good things about you professionally from people whose opinions I respected. So when I was looking for the Lozier Girl, you were the obvious choice.'

'How very convenient for you!' she snapped, her eyes flashing fire.

'Not really.' He was leaning back against the gunwale of the boat, watching her with that cool, enigmatic gaze she found so disconcerting. 'As a general rule I prefer not to go to bed with a model while I'm working with her—it can cause all sorts of unwelcome complications.'

'Oh . . .?' Her heart had begun to pound, and her mouth was dry.

'But on this occasion,' he added, those smoky eyes mocking her, 'I think I could make an exception.'

CHAPTER SEVEN

THE afternoon light had that vivid clarity that could only be found this close to the equator. The pale coral sand crunched between Alysha's toes, and the warm breeze drifting in from the sea fanned her cheeks. Wearing a light cotton kimono-style wrap, she was waiting for Ross to finish setting up his camera.

At last he straightened, satisfied. 'OK—are you ready?'

She nodded, her mouth dry. She wasn't ready—she would never be ready... She could no longer even pretend to herself that the only reason they were here was to take the shots for the campaign. Her fingers were clumsy as she fumbled to untie the belt of her wrap.

He glanced back at her, and she was almost relieved to see the signs of his characteristic impatience; at least while he was working he was working, her naked body no more than a shape in his camera lens. 'Come on, hurry up. Have you got plenty of sun-block on?'

'Of... course,' she managed a little unsteadily.

'On your back too?'

'As much of it as I could reach,' she retorted, unable to control the edginess in her voice.

He shook his head, his mouth a hard line of exasperation. 'That won't do—you'll have missed patches. I don't want you getting sunburned—that wouldn't be much of a recommendation for the product. I'd better rub some more on for you.'

'No, thank you!' she protested a little too quickly.

'Don't argue. Stay there.'

She rolled her fine eyes heavenwards. 'Where else can I go?' she murmured in wry resignation.

He conceded a laugh, and went to fetch the tube of sun-block from the dinghy they had used to bring in the equipment from the yacht.

She waited, her eyes unfocused as she gazed out at the distant horizon. A painful honesty forced her to admit that she had known when she had agreed to come here with him, alone like this, what it was bound to lead to. Would it really have been so bad to have had the rest of the crew here? After all, they were all professionals; they would have worked on shoots like this any number of times.

So why *had* she chosen to come alone with Ross? Maybe, she acknowledged with a trace of bitter irony, because she had been harbouring some kind of foolish, romantic dream that making love and falling in love were the same thing; but that dream had been shattered by his brutally unvarnished statement of fact. To him, it was a basic, physical act—he saw no need for any emotion. If she allowed herself to succumb now, she would only have herself to blame when he broke her heart—as he certainly would.

She tensed as she heard the scrunch of his returning footsteps across the sand.

'Are you going to take your wrap off?' he enquired, an inflection of sardonic humour in his voice.

'Oh... Yes, of course...' She drew in a deep, steadying breath, and unfastened the belt. She had turned her back to him, but it didn't really help; a shiver of nervous trepidation feathered down the length of her spine as she slipped the wrap back from her shoulders, snatching it off quickly and clutching it in front of her like some kind of shield.

'Pull your hair out of the way,' he commanded briskly.

She did as he ordered, holding herself proudly erect and refusing to let herself flinch away as he stroked the cool cream across her bare back. His touch was firm and sure, sliding smoothly across her naked skin, tracing a tantalising path down the long curve of her spine and caressing with lingering care the soft, feminine roundness of her *derrière*.

He would make love like that, she found herself thinking—with an assured expertise that would leave a woman melting helplessly in his arms. The images filled her brain, driving out all rational thought. What did it matter what happened afterwards? She no longer cared—she wanted him so much, she would take him on whatever terms he was prepared to offer...

'OK—shall we begin?'

She drew in a sharp breath. The photographs—he was talking about the photographs... With an effort of will, she pulled herself together; they had a job to do—that was primarily why they were here. Moving across to the spot he was indicating, she dropped her wrap just out of shot, and kneeled down gracefully in the sand, her back to him. He was right about the composition, at least, she reflected with reluctant admiration—it was perfect.

'Right. Shake back your hair—that's it. Put your hands underneath it and lift it away from your shoulders...'

Alysha obeyed his instructions, trying hard to focus on producing the best possible set of pictures, and to forget her nakedness. It wasn't easy—even with her back to him, she felt exposed and vulnerable... though she couldn't deny that it was a deeply sensual feeling, arousing a primeval core of feminine submissiveness inside her that she had never known she possessed.

The moist tropical heat simmered around them as they worked. Between them they devised every variation on the pose imaginable; kneeling in the sand, she would tip her head back, shaking her hair so that it danced in the sunlight; sitting cross-legged, she stretched her arms above her head, lacing her hands together; lying on her stomach, propped on her elbows, she let the warm wavelets ripple around her, glancing back over her shoulder to slant an enigmatic smile into the camera lens.

It was more than an hour before he was finally satisfied. 'OK, that's fine,' he pronounced at last as the whir of the automatic winder signalled the end of the roll of film. 'Let's take a break.' He picked up her wrap and tossed it to her. 'Here. I could do with another drink.'

'So could I,' Alysha agreed readily. She shrugged her slim shoulders into the wrap as she rose to her feet, tying the belt loosely around her waist, and followed him up the beach to the shelter of a tall coconut palm, throwing herself down in the sand with a sigh of relief.

They had brought a cool-box from the yacht, and he took out two cans of cola, passing one to her. She leaned back against the trunk of the tree, closing her eyes and tipping her head back to swallow a long, welcome draught of the ice-cold fizz.

The click of a camera brought her eyes open—Ross was taking her picture again. She laughed in wry resignation—there really was no point in objecting.

'That's great!' he approved. 'You look fabulous.'

She was a little startled. Not once while they had been working had he given her a word of praise—yet now, while she was relaxing, the faded old robe falling anyhow around her, a bead of sweat trickling down the side of her cheek, he was impressed.

'I must look a wreck,' she protested, shaking her head.

The camera clicked again, catching the movement of her hair. 'Don't stop,' he insisted in urgent encouragement, prowling around her to find another angle. 'Keep doing it for me.'

Wryly conceding, she slipped into the spirit of it, wiping the cold can across her forehead, putting out her lower lip to blow cool air up over her face, fanning herself with the loose lapels of her wrap. 'You're surely not planning to use these in the campaign?' she questioned on a note of incredulous amusement.

He shook his head, his eyes glinting darkly. 'Not these,' he responded, dropping on to one knee to catch her profile against the vivid blue of the sky. 'God, you look so sexy sitting there like that.'

She laughed in astonishment. Sexy? He had to be crazy! When she was sweltering in the late afternoon heat, her hair draggled and her golden skin beaded with sweat? And yet . . . it was true; maybe it was the lush beauty of their surroundings, or maybe it was the seductive persuasion of that soft, husky voice, with its beguiling trace of unpolished Glaswegian accent, but something strange had taken hold of her, an unfamiliar spirit of wantonness that was prompting her into behaviour that was completely out of character.

The wrap had fallen loose, and she knew that from that angle the honeyed curve of one firm breast was almost completely visible to him. But she didn't try to cover it; instead she slanted him a mischievously come-hither glance from beneath her lashes, bending up one knee to deliberately expose the slender length of her thigh.

'That's it—give me more,' he coaxed, focusing in for a close-up as she ran the moist tip of her tongue over the soft fullness of her parted lips. 'Sensational...'

Caught up in the spell, it seemed as though she was someone else, some daring, provocative creature who knew how to tease and entice. In one small sane corner of her mind she knew that it was crazy to let him take such pictures of her, but events were already spinning way beyond her control.

Trailing her fingertips down the edge of her wrap, she drew it back a little further to offer him a tantalising glimpse of the soft shadow between her breasts. He had squatted down on his haunches in front of her, and as if under the compulsion of those glittering grey eyes she unfastened the tie belt, letting the wrap slip back from her shoulders—and then, drawing in a long, deep breath, she let it drop, uncovering the ripe curve of her naked breasts, the rosy pink nipples hardened into taut buds, pert and inviting.

The camera clicked rapidly, capturing her flagrant exhibition. But she didn't care; she was enjoying his reaction, exhilarated by this confirmation that she had the power to arouse his genuine admiration. She lifted her hands behind her head, so that her breasts rose proudly, and then, straddling her bare legs wide apart, she burrowed her fingers into the crisp white sand between them, laughing provocatively into the dark lens.

'That's incredible,' he breathed. 'Absolutely superb...'

Standing up, she turned her back on him, letting the loose wrap trail on the ground so that the full length of her spine, and the soft curve of her *derrière*, were left naked. Then she let the wrap fall, and hugged the slender trunk of the tree, pouting at him over her shoulder.

'Now turn around,' he commanded softly.

Her heart was pounding, making her feel a little dizzy, but the spell that had caught her was too powerful to resist. She turned to face him, leaning back against the tree, her tawny eyes hot as they gazed into his. For one long, tense moment they both stood there, as the whole world seemed to fall still, waiting.

He wasn't even pretending to look at her with a professional eye; his gaze slid slowly down over her naked curves, lingering hungrily over the ripe, firm swell of her breasts, succulently tipped with pink; over the peach-smooth curve of her stomach, dimpled by her dainty navel. And then on, to fix on the soft dusky crest of curls that crowned her slender thighs.

She seemed to be melting sweetly in the heat of that intimate survey, her body responding as if he was caressing her. He smiled, a sensuous promise, and lifted his camera again, firing off shot after shot as she posed for him exactly as she had vowed she never would.

The whir of the auto-wind signalled the end of the film. Alysha caught her breath, waiting tensely as with the habitual care of the professional he removed the film and dropped it into a spare canister, and then put the camera carefully back into its steel case, closing it to keep out the sand.

And then he turned back to her, those smoky eyes glinting with unmistakable intent. She felt the muscles of her stomach tighten in apprehension, but as he came towards her she couldn't move away. This had always been inevitable, from the very beginning...

He came close, but didn't touch her; she could feel the heat of his body, radiating across the inches between them. He hadn't put his T-shirt on again after his earlier swim, and that intriguingly masculine pelt of hair across his wide chest held her mesmerised; the temptation to trail her fingertips through it was now too strong to resist.

A warning tremor of response ran through him at her touch; his skin was warm, and she could feel the powerful thud of his heartbeat beneath his ribs. Lifting her eyes slowly, she gazed up into his; it seemed as though a dark, hypnotic fire was smouldering in their depths—a fire that would burn away all memory of her past, all care for her future.

He put out one hand, stroking it down her quivering flank and round over the smooth curve of her *derrière* to rest over the base of her spine; and then with an abrupt movement he dragged her against him, making her devastatingly aware of the powerful surge of his hard male arousal. Her eyes widened in shock; how would she ever...?

With a low groan his mouth came down on hers, crushing her lips apart, his sensuous tongue invading forcefully the sweet depths within, plundering ruthlessly every secret corner. And she could only respond, surrendering herself totally to his savage demand, her tender breasts and taut, sensitised nipples chafed by the rough pelt of dark curls across his hard chest as he moulded her naked body intimately against his hard length.

His hands were tangled in her hair, pushing it back from her face as his kisses trailed a scalding path across her trembling eyelids, the racing pulse beneath her temple, to swirl into the delicate shell of her ear, his hard teeth nibbling at her lobe and the hot tip of his tongue finding the delicious spot behind it, making her shiver as if in a fever.

Her head had tipped back, and she could hear her own breathing, ragged and husky; her bones had melted, and she could only cling to him, her pliant body curved against the hard length of his as his hand slid down over her silken skin to lift and encompass the aching fullness of one ripe breast, crushing it beneath his palm, his clever fingers pinching and teasing the sweet, tender bud of her nipple to dart sparks of fire into her brain.

He leaned her back against the rough trunk of the tree, his feet braced between hers to hold them apart, and as his hand stroked down over her smooth stomach to tangle into that downy crest of curls that crowned her thighs she realised with a quick little flutter of panic that she had no way of defending the vulnerable cleft between.

But the touch of his fingers was light, magical, exploring delicately into the moist warmth, parting the soft velvet folds to seek the tiny seed-pearl concealed within. A shaft of pure pleasure shot through her, making her gasp, her spine curling in ecstasy, and he laughed softly, mockingly.

'God, you're a sexy little thing,' he growled. 'You put on that demure act, pretending to be oh, so chaste and ladylike—but this is what you've been wanting all along, isn't it?'

She struggled to deny the accusation, but all that emerged from her lips was a helpless little moan. She closed her eyes, dark fires swirling around her as he laid her down in the warm sand. Instinctively she reached up for him, wrapping her arms around him and drawing him down to her, her lips parting hungrily to welcome his plundering kiss, her body moving beneath his in urgent supplication.

He laughed again, chiding her haste. 'Such flattering eagerness,' he murmured teasingly. 'But there's no hurry—we have two long nights and days to enjoy each other. I've waited five years for this. I used to look at that batch of photographs, and imagine what it would be like to feel you in my arms again. Now that I have you, I'm not going to rush it—I intend to savour every exquisite moment.'

And he did, as she lay helpless beneath him, her body a sweet sacrifice to his carnal appetites. Her breasts ached beneath the tormenting brush of his kisses, the rosy nipples a raw focus of nerve-endings that throbbed beneath his touch as he teased and nipped at them, his hot, rough tongue swirling around them, until at last his lips closed over first one, and then the other, suckling them with a deep, hungry rhythm that pulsed fire through her veins.

She was lost in a world of pure sensation, swept up in the current of desire that was raging through her. His hand had slid down to stroke smoothly over the silken flesh of her inner thighs as she parted them compliantly, aching for a renewal of those magical intimate caresses.

A ragged sob escaped her throat as his clever fingers found again that secret nub of pleasure, stroking it into the most exquisite, electric arousal. Never had she dreamed that she could be capable of feeling such a fierce, uncontrollable need, or of responding with such unbridled rapture.

Some small part of her mind was still appalled at her own wanton behaviour; he wasn't even pretending to offer any more than this brief interlude—in two days it would be over, and he would go back to Barbara as if nothing had happened. To him, this was no more than a casual encounter, probably one of many he enjoyed—with Barbara's tacit permission or without it.

How could she have so little respect for herself, to allow herself to be used like this? But though she knew it could only lead to painful regret, it was far too late to turn back. Looking down at his dark head moving over her naked body, she felt only a warm tide of feminine submissiveness; her heart was his to break as casually as he wished.

He was tasting every inch of her honeyed skin; his tongue swirled sensuously into the dainty dip of her navel, making her shiver with heat, and then trailed on, meandering down across her stomach, and as her eyes widened in shock his head bent between her parted thighs, and she realised that the magic of his skilful fingers was nothing to the havoc the hot lap of his tongue could wreak on that exquisitely sensitised nub of pleasure.

It was a blissful agony that had her writhing in torment, her spine a quivering arc; she could hear her own voice crying out, pleading in desperate entreaty for the fulfillment of his hard possession. The torrid heat of the late afternoon simmered around them, slicking their bodies with sweat, as the blue crystal waters lapped in soft, caressing rhythm against the white coral sand.

She felt his weight shift as he moved to lie above her, lifting himself on his bunched biceps, his hard thighs coaxing hers wider apart. She opened misted eyes to gaze up into his face; at this moment of ultimate surrender she wanted to look at him, to etch the memory indelibly into her mind so that she could relive it long after he had wandered on to pastures new.

I love you. But she kept the words inside her head; let him believe that for her, too, this was no more than a physical thing, the satisfaction of a basic appetite, of no greater significance than eating or drinking. 'Love' and 'forever' would only complicate things unnecessarily.

With an effort of will, she fought the instinct to tense as she felt the nudge of his rigid shaft against the delicate folds of velvet; if it was to hurt, it was a pain she would willingly accept. But she wasn't ready for the shock as he thrust deep into her. An involuntary cry broke from her lips, and her spine arched rigidly.

He stared down at her, an expression of absolute astonishment on his face. But then to her surprise he began to laugh in what was unmistakably delight, holding her tightly and covering her face with kisses.

'My God! I'm sorry—I didn't mean to hurt you. I
didn't know—I would never have guessed... Why
didn't you tell me?'

'You...don't mind?' she queried a little shakily.

'Mind? Of course not—why should I?'

'Oh, just...I thought...you'd be expecting me to
have...a little more experience.'

He chuckled in rich amusement, shaking his head.
'Don't worry about experience,' he asserted on a
husky growl. 'I can provide you with plenty of that.
What I *hadn't* expected was the privilege of taking
your virginity—in these days, and in the world we
work in, it must be almost unique.'

She had to lower her lashes to veil her eyes, afraid
that he would see in them the truth of what was in
her heart—a truth that wouldn't be welcome to him.
'It...just wasn't something I'd got around to yet,'
she murmured, struggling to convey an air of casual
unconcern. 'But I suppose it was bound to happen
sooner or later.'

That hard mouth took on a cynical twist. 'Then
I'm glad I was in the right place at the right time,' he
responded, the faintly sardonic edge in his tone
making her wonder if she had overplayed her act a
little. 'And I can certainly assure you that I shall do
everything in my power—*everything*——' his eyes
glinted with wicked pleasure as he began to move
slowly inside her '—to ensure that the next few days
provide you with the kind of satisfaction the occasion
warrants.'

She could only believe him. At first he was so gentle,
holding back the powerful forces that she could sense
smouldering inside him so as to give her time to adjust
to the newness of what was happening to her. But as

he was sure that she was all right, he began to build the rhythm, coaxing her to match his movements, and she found that magically all trace of that fleeting pain had vanished, to be replaced by the most exquisite ripples of sensation deep in the pit of her stomach.

And then he began to increase the pace, varying the rhythm with deeper, more powerful thrusts, moving in grinding circles to stretch her deliciously, his hands sliding beneath her to lift her to meet the full force of his demand. She could only cling to him, following his lead as best she could, the sound of her own ragged breathing and racing pulse in her ears, all her senses focused on the sweet pleasure that was flooding through her.

The temperature was rising, surging out of control; caught up in the dizzying vortex, Alysha heard herself crying out, her body thrashing and arching in ecstatic spasms as Ross pounded into her, all restraint forgotten. And then at last he tensed, exploding in a shuddering climax, to collapse into her arms, all that magnificent power spent.

She was crushed beneath his weight, but she didn't mind. She held him, marvelling at the helplessness of that big, hard body—a helplessness she had induced. All the jagged tension inside her had been released, to be replaced by a honeyed glow that had spread through all her limbs, leaving her feeling languid and totally at peace. It no longer mattered what the future might hold—she belonged to him, totally and irrevocably.

After a time he stirred, mumbling an apology for being so heavy, and shifting to one side he drew her close, to lie nestled into the crook of his arm. 'Are you all right?' he asked gently.

'Of course.' Now was the critical moment—it would be so easy to yield to the temptation to tell him that she loved him, to beg him to make promises she knew she had no right to ask. He had made it quite clear that all he wanted was a...brief physical encounter—she still winced at the memory of the blunt word he had used. She would have to exert every ounce of will-power, every ounce of acting skill she possessed, and pretend that that was all she had wanted too. 'Fancy another Coke?' she enquired lightly.

'I want to eat,' he retorted, slapping her dainty rump as she rose gracefully to her feet. 'Sex makes me hungry.'

'All right.' She forced herself to ignore that casual reference to the many occasions when he had enjoyed this intimate afterglow with other women. 'What would you like?'

'Smoked salmon and caviar,' he declared, yawning luxuriously and stretching his long, powerful limbs in the sand. 'Nothing less could match the occasion.'

'You're greedy,' she teased, secretly delighted at the oblique compliment.

'I know.' He grinned up at her mischievously. 'Want to know how much?' He reached out and caught her hand, dragging her down into the sand and rolling on top of her—and she gasped in shock as she recognised the proof of his unabated appetite. She hadn't yet fully recovered from their first encounter—her breasts tingled with raw sensitivity, her thighs ached. If he made love to her again so soon, she wouldn't be able to stand up!

'I...I'd better go back to the boat and see what there is to eat,' she protested, wriggling out from beneath him.

He laughed teasingly, recognising her apprehension, but he let her go.

They wouldn't be working any more this
afternoon—the sun would soon be setting—so she
didn't have to worry about getting her hair wet.
Leaving the dinghy, she waded out a little way into
the cool water, and then with a graceful dive slid beneath the surface, only coming up when she reached
the yacht.

That brief immersion had at least cooled her blood
a little, bringing her back to her senses. She must have
been crazy to let herself give in to temptation like that!
And yet . . . somehow she couldn't regret it. Though
she knew that it had meant little to him, it had been
for her a brief glimpse of paradise that she would
cherish for the rest of her life.

Hauling herself up on to the swimming-platform
at the stern of the yacht, she paused to wring the sea-
water out of her hair, and then climbed aboard. There
were towels in the cupboard built in behind the aft
bulkhead, and she found a large one to wrap sarong-
style around her body, and another to make a turban
for her hair, and then went down to the galley to in-
vestigate what had been provided in the way of food.

There was more than enough for a banquet: smoked
salmon and lobster, chicken wings and spare ribs,
kebabs of lamb and beef, tubs of Thai vegetables, all
cooked and frozen, ready to pop in the microwave,
as well as masses of fresh, ripe fruit—mangoes and
papaya and rambutans, jack-fruits, and the strong-
smelling but delicious durian.

She was setting the meal out on the table when Ross
came in; he had returned in the dinghy, bringing his
camera and equipment back with him. She glanced

up as he clambered over the gunwale, relieved to see that at least he had put his shorts on.

'Mmm—looks good,' he approved, coming up behind her and sliding his arms around her waist, drawing her back against him. 'I'm ravenous—must be all the fresh air.'

She slanted him a crooked smile. 'Well, there's certainly no shortage of food.'

He laughed, nuzzling into the sensitive hollows of her shoulder. 'It was ordered for half a dozen,' he reminded her, letting his hands slide up to mould the ripe fullness of her breasts through the thick layer of towelling that covered them. 'We'll just have to manage as best we can.'

He reached out and picked up a spicy beef satay, gnawing on it with his strong white teeth as he continued to caress her breast almost casually, a slight tensing of his muscles warning her that he wasn't going to let her escape until he felt so inclined.

'What have you put this thing on for?' he demanded, tugging at the towel. 'You can't possibly be cold.'

'No, but . . . I thought we were going to eat,' she countered, her voice unsteady as she responded helplessly to what he was doing to her.

'Take it off,' he growled insistently. 'I want to look at you naked.'

'You've been looking at me all afternoon,' she protested, her cheeks tinged with pink as she tried to hold the towel in place.

'So I want to look at you some more.' With a flick of his wrist he dragged it off her, snatching it away as she tried to grab at it. 'That's better,' he approved, his eyes ruthlessly raking down over her naked body.

'Beautiful—every inch. Your skin is like pure silk. And your breasts are perfect: as firm and ripe as peaches, with the prettiest little pink nipples I've ever seen.'

She flashed him a look of sharp annoyance; his words might be flattering, but to her they only underlined the painful fact that he saw her purely as an object of physical pleasure, her value based solely on the fortuitous lineaments of her face and body.

He laughed softly, mocking her anger. 'What's wrong?'

She shrugged her slender shoulders in wry resignation; there was really no point in trying to cover herself up now, she acknowledged bitterly—it was a little late for such modesty. She moved away from him, sliding in behind the table and curling her legs up beneath her on the soft leather-upholstered bench seat that ran along the side of the cabin.

'What did...Gemma say when you told her we were coming here together?' she enquired tautly.

He lifted one dark eyebrow in lazy question, betraying no hint of conscience at the mention of the other girl's name. 'Why should she say anything?' he countered coolly, sitting down opposite her and glancing over the food, making a considered selection to pile on to his plate.

Her eyes glittered with frost. 'Do you always conduct your affairs like this?' she demanded.

'Like what?'

She slanted him a searching look from beneath her lashes. 'Like...this. You're having an affair with Bobbie, and then there was Gemma, and now you're here with me, like this...'

He returned her a look of mild amusement. 'You make me sound like some kind of Bluebeard,' he teased.

'But you're not denying it?' she challenged.

He shrugged his wide shoulders in a gesture of lazy indifference. 'Would you believe me if I did?'

'No, I wouldn't,' she asserted, stung by his dismissive attitude—though she really shouldn't have been surprised by it.

That fascinating mouth curved into a smile of sardonic amusement. 'You know, if anyone were listening to this conversation, they could be forgiven for thinking you were my wife,' he remarked drily.

'Your *wife*?' Her heart kicked hard against her ribs, and she had to struggle with every atom of skill she possessed to maintain some semblance of her cool façade. 'I hardly think so.'

He laughed coldly. 'Then it's rather fortunate that I have no plans to ask you, isn't it?' he returned, a steely glint in those grey eyes. 'I'm good enough to gain a little sexual experience with, but not to take home to Mummy, eh? But do you know what always fascinates me about well-bred young ladies like you?' he added, regarding her with faintly sneering contempt. 'They can take longer to get warmed up, but once they start they're far wilder than any of the others.'

'Oh, really?' She reached out for a chicken kebab, struggling to retain some semblance of dignity; even if they weren't quarrelling she would have felt awkward, sitting there like that with no clothes on. But now it almost seemed as if he was punishing her, deliberately letting his eyes linger over the firm, ripe curves of her naked breasts as he calmly ate his meal.

'Yes, really.' He put down the chunk of bread roll he had been eating, the warning glint in his eyes making her heart thud in alarm. 'Like me to prove it to you?'

'No, I . . . don't think that will be necessary,' she protested unsteadily, edging back into the corner of the seat.

He laughed, huskily mocking, and with a swift movement leaned round the table, catching her ankle and dragging her out from her retreat. 'No?' he taunted, capturing her wrists and jerking her ruthlessly to her feet. 'Do you know what I think?' he remarked, those hard grey eyes alight with mocking amusement. 'I think you're a stuck-up little madam who deserves to be taken down a peg or two. And I know just how to do it.'

'Let me go!' she protested, struggling furiously to escape from him. 'I won't let you make love to me again!'

'Oh, I wasn't planning to make love to you,' he murmured, drawing her inexorably close against him, wrapping her arms around behind her own back and arching her spine so that her naked breasts brushed tantalisingly against the hard wall of his chest. 'That's far too genteel and refined a term for what I have in mind.'

On a surge of hot anger, she kicked him on the shin, breaking his hold and darting free of him to scramble up on to the deck. But there was nowhere to go—except over the side. As he followed her from the cabin she backed away from him, breathless—and then with a swift movement she picked up a cushion from the sun-lounger and threw it at him, delaying him just long enough to allow her to swing herself over the rail and dive out into the warm crystal water.

A splash behind her warned that he was close, and she struck out strongly for the beach, but he quickly overhauled her, capturing her in the shallows as she tried to run and tumbling her into the soft, wet sand at the water's edge. He was laughing, exhilarated by the chase, and she glared up at him in fury, still kicking and fighting.

'You bastard! I hate you! Let me go!'

But her voice lacked conviction, and as he knelt across her, catching both her hands and pinning them back into the sand behind her head, subduing her struggles with ease, they both knew that she was going to be able to offer no more than a token resistance.

CHAPTER EIGHT

'I DON'T know—it really doesn't seem a bit like Christmas.' Audrey Fordham-Jones sighed for what must have been at least the sixth time.

Oliver glanced up from his book, and slanted Alysha a mischievous wink. 'The Queen's speech'll be on in a minute,' he remarked helpfully.

'Not for almost half an hour,' his mother responded with dismal pessimism. 'And then it's nothing but those awful game-shows. They never seem to put a decent film on these days.'

Alysha rose to her feet. 'I'll make a cup of tea,' she suggested, as much as an excuse to escape from the room as because she wanted one.

Christmas... No, it didn't seem much like Christmas. A six-foot tree, decked out with tinsel and fairy-lights, a dozen or so Christmas cards set out on the sideboard, and a brave holly-wreath on the front door, seemed almost to mock the lack of festive spirit in the house.

Maybe it was the weather—dull, grey, wintry drizzle, instead of the pretty drifts of snow the Christmas cards portrayed. Or maybe it was just because she and Oliver were grown-up now, no longer excited by the prospect of brightly wrapped presents and iced Christmas cake.

But it wasn't even that which was making her feel so low, she acknowledged wryly, gazing out of the kitchen window at the wet, bedraggled garden. Was it really only forty-eight hours since she had got back from Thailand? Those few sparkling, magical days she had spent with Ross seemed now as if they had been no more than a dream, a time outside the mundane course of the world—it was hard even to believe that that idyllic tropical paradise could be on the same planet.

They hadn't seen another living soul all the time they were there—not even a boat on the horizon. Living like castaways, they had hardly bothered with clothes at all—occasionally Alysha would wrap a simple sarong around her hips, and Ross might pull on those faded and cut-down chinos, but most of the time it had seemed more natural simply to walk around naked.

They hadn't forgotten that they were there to work, of course—and Ross had made her work as hard as ever; stylishly posed on the sea-washed rocks, like a mermaid, half turned from the camera with her arm discreetly concealing the curve of her breast, or swimming beneath the clear crystal waters as he leaned out over the gunwale of the boat, a polarising filter over the camera lens to refract the glare of the sun.

But those weren't the only photographs he had taken: others were far more intimate—shots of her rolling around naked in the sand at the water's edge, the rippling waves playing over her body as she laughed up into the camera's eye, shots of her relaxing in a string hammock slung between a couple of tall palm trees on the beach, shots of her draped languidly across the rocks, the soft, ripe contours of her breasts, stomach and thighs outlined against the vivid blue sky.

And they had made love. Alysha had found it hard to recognise herself in this wanton creature she had become, so greedy for her lover's body, so willing to learn all he could teach her about the arts of erotic pleasure. And it had seemed as though he, too, could never get enough of her; he seemed to enjoy just looking at her, but very often a look would lead to a casual caress, and then he would pull her into his arms and the fires would flare between them again, as hot as the very first time.

She had tried not to think too much about Barbara, or Gemma. Perhaps the gossips had been wrong, after all—though he hadn't actually denied any of it. She couldn't quite bring herself to press him on the subject—she preferred to live only in the present, pretending to herself that this fragile illusion would last forever.

But of course, like all things, it had to come to an end. They had returned the yacht to Ko Samui, and taken the short flight up to Bangkok together. From there, Ross was flying on to Australia, where he would be spending Christmas with Tina, his studio assistant at the time they had first met, while she was returning straight home...

The departure lounge was crowded—hardly the place to say goodbye. Ross hadn't spoken of the future at all, and she daren't let herself ask—if he thought she was trying to pressure him into a commitment he would run a mile. No, if this was to be the end of their brief affair, she was determined to say goodbye with dry eyes. She had rehearsed the words so much that by the time she had to say them they came out stiff and flat.

'Well . . . I'll see you around, then.'

A flicker of sardonic humour lit those cool grey eyes. 'Of course you will,' he responded. 'You're under contract to me, remember?'

'Of course.' She held out her hand—it was only shaking slightly—and managed something that resembled a smile. 'Have a good journey.'

'Thank you.' He took her hand, but instead of shaking it he drew her inexorably into his arms. 'And the same to you.'

She recognised his intent, and tried to draw back— a quick peck on the cheek might be appropriate, but not a major clinch, not in front of all these people.

He chuckled with mocking laughter. 'Don't fight me,' he warned softly. 'Not unless you want everyone to stare.'

'Ross . . .!' But her protest was smothered as his mouth came down on hers, claiming a kiss of the most flagrant intimacy. His hand slid slowly down the length of her spine to mould her shockingly close to him, as his tongue plundered languorously into every sweet, secret corner of her mouth, igniting the responses he had come to know so well.

By the time he finally let her go she was breathless and blushing, her neatly coiled hair tousled and her immaculate lipstick smudged. 'You wretch!' she grumbled, darting a swift, embarrassed glance around. 'Just look at the state of me.'

'I'm looking,' he teased. 'You look all right to me.'

'I shall have to . . . Oh, there's the last call for my flight—I have to hurry . . .!'

'Don't panic,' he coaxed, catching her around the waist again. 'They won't be closing the gate just yet. Why do you want to dash back to England anyway?

It's nothing but rain and gales. Why don't you change your ticket and come on to Sydney with me? Tina'd be happy to put you up. We can spend Christmas on Bondi Beach, surfing and having a barbie. Among other things,' he added, a wicked glint in his smiling eyes.

She stared up at him, startled. The suggestion had come completely out of the blue—he hadn't given her time to think... 'I... can't,' she protested haltingly, 'I promised to go home for Christmas. My family will be expecting me.'

'Call them—tell them you're not coming. You're a big girl now—you don't have to do what your parents want all the time.'

Her tawny eyes flashed in angry indignation. It was typical of him to regard such a promise so lightly—to be broken at the slightest whim. Of course it was very tempting to agree; perhaps if he hadn't made it quite so explicit that the invitation was prompted mainly by a desire to prolong their sexual encounter she might have succumbed.

But if she went along with him, how long would it be before he found her availability boring, cheating on her as he was now cheating on Barbara, discarding her as carelessly as he had discarded Gemma? Alastair's wise warning came back into her mind; 'Always keep him wanting just that little bit more than you're giving.'

'No.' She shook her head firmly. 'I'm sorry, but I'm not going to break my promise. Besides, I'm not going out of duty—I like spending Christmas with my family. Don't you?'

'I don't have any family,' he countered abruptly.

She glanced up at him in surprise, her anger evaporating; that bleak statement had opened a rare glimpse into his life, betraying a hurt she knew instinctively he never willingly revealed. She wanted to reach out and soothe the pain, but he had already released her from his embrace, his smile hard and mocking.

'Well, you'd better go, then,' he said. 'You don't want to miss your plane.'

'Ross...' But it was too late to say anything; as he pushed her away she found herself caught up in the last-minute stampede for the gate, which carried her through and away from him, and when she looked around to wave goodbye he had already disappeared...

If only she had gone with him... What was he doing, right at this moment? Picnicking on some glorious golden beach, beneath a hot southern sun? But in fact it would be the middle of the night in Australia, she amended with a touch of wry humour—he would be in bed. Alone? It didn't seem very likely, not on past form. Maybe he was even with Tina; he had claimed that she was now happily married—but then he would say that, wouldn't he?

If only she had gone with him...

Briskly she shook her head. She had made the right choice, she had to keep reminding herself of that. After all, he would be home soon, and then... well, then she would find out if he was still interested. And if he was, would it be wise to let their affair continue?

No, it wouldn't; but unfortunately, when you fell in love, wisdom seemed to be the first thing to fly out of the window. She had even found herself hoping that she might be pregnant. Foolishly, perhaps, that possibility hadn't even occurred to her while they were on the island; but then it hadn't occurred to Ross either, apparently—at least he had shown no concern about taking any precautions.

Just this morning, she had found out that she wasn't. Of course she was relieved—a pregnancy would have been a disaster at this point in her career, and heaven only knew how she would have managed financially. And she didn't care to dwell on what Ross's reaction was likely to have been. But on the other hand, a baby... Ross's baby...

She turned as the door opened, smiling in guilty relief that it was her brother rather than her mother who appeared. 'The tea's nearly ready,' she informed him breezily. 'Want another slice of cake?'

He shook his head with a grimace. 'Ugh—no. It's ghastly. Where did she get it from?'

'She made it herself. For heaven's sake don't let on that you don't like it—she'd be so disappointed.'

'Lord!' he gasped. 'It's a good job you warned me! I suppose I'd better have some—I can always take something for the indigestion afterwards.'

She chuckled with laughter. 'Oh, it's not that bad. And it's good that she's making the effort—we ought to encourage her.'

'Hmph!' He slanted her a rueful grin. 'Actually, I wasn't going to come home at all this Christmas,' he confessed. 'I was going to stay with Nige. It was only the thought of how rotten it'd be for you, having to cope with her on your own, that made me change my mind.'

She smiled wryly. 'Actually, I nearly didn't come myself. I was... thinking of spending it in Australia.'

'Oh?' Oliver, unfortunately, had a remarkably sharp memory, and since she had briefly mentioned earlier that it was to Australia that Ross had gone he was very swiftly able to put two and two together. 'It's more than just business with you two, then?' he enquired.

A faint tinge of pink coloured her cheeks. 'No, of course not,' she responded a little too quickly. 'It was just... I mean, it wasn't...'

'Oliver? Alysha? Come along, hurry up—the Queen's speech is about to start.'

Brother and sister exchanged glances of sardonic humour. Alysha picked up the tea-tray, while Oliver held open the door for her. 'Ah—now it's beginning to seem like Christmas,' he murmured, making her giggle.

Paris in January was cold. Even though the sun was shining weakly in the washed-out sky, a silver dusting of frost still traced the bare branches of the tall trees along the banks of the Seine. Alysha caught a glimpse of the high white roofs and graceful buttresses of Notre dame as the taxi swept across the bridge to the Left Bank, and turned into the fashionable district of St Germain.

Paris—city of love. But not for her; she was simply here to work—one frantic week of fittings, and then it would be straight into the chaotic whirl of the *haute couture* collections. Love... that was just an illusion.

She had neither seen nor heard from Ross since they had parted in Bangkok—she didn't even know if he had returned from Australia. Not that she had expected much, of course—but surely he could have at

least managed a telephone call to wish her a happy
New Year...?

If only she could be more like Barbara, she reflected wryly; it had taken her very little time to re-
cover from any heartache she might have suffered at
Ross Elliot's hands—on New Year's Eve she had announced her engagement to Sir Richard Maynard, the
chairman of Loziers!

The taxi turned into one of the small cobbled
squares close to the Jardin du Luxembourg, and came
to a halt before the entrance to a smart hotel. Alysha
glanced up at it in some surprise; the agency had
booked it for her, but she hadn't expected it to be
quite so upmarket. Tall and elegant, of mellow golden
stone, it had graceful wrought-iron balconies at all
the windows, and a pair of neatly clipped bay-trees
in wooden tubs flanking the wide front doors.

But it was certainly the right place. A polite
concierge in dark green livery stepped forward to open
the door for her, and with the collar of her stylish
trench-coat turned up against the damp she wasted
no time in darting from the warmth of the taxi to the
warmth of the reception.

Inside it had a discreet *fin-de-siècle* splendour, all
bronzed glass and gleaming amber burr-walnut, and
soft golden lighting shed from elegant Lalique globes.
The distinguished-looking gentleman behind the desk
looked as if he could have dated from the same era.
He greeted her with a formal little bow.

'*Ah oui*, Mademoiselle Jones. Welcome to Paris. I
trust you had a pleasant journey? It is rather cold, is
it not?' As she signed the register, he rang a small
silver bell on his desk to summon a smart young bell-
boy. 'Jean-Claude will show you to your room. I trust

you will have a very pleasant stay. *Jean-Claude, suite trois-quatorze,*' he instructed briskly. '*Viens.*'

Alysha thanked him, and followed the bell-boy into an antique wrought-iron lift, that rose with majestic contempt for modern hustle to the third floor—Alysha could have walked up the stairs that spiralled around it in half the time, but such precipitate behaviour would have seemed the most appalling solecism in these elegant surroundings.

The corridor that they came to was long, with doors that gleamed with generations of beeswax opening off each side of it. The thick, wine-red carpet muffled every sound. At intervals along the walls were set some rather good pieces of antique French furniture, adding to the impression that she was in the private home of some cultured aristocrat rather than a hotel.

Suite three-fourteen was the last one on the right, and Alysha sought swiftly in her handbag for an appropriate tip as the bell-boy tapped on the door.

Her brain must have been working rather slowly this afternoon; it had just occurred to her to wonder why he was *knocking* on the door, instead of using his pass-key, when someone inside opened it—and Paris inexplicably entered the earthquake zone.

'Ross...?'

Those steel-grey eyes glinted in amusement, mocking her astonishment. 'Hello, darling. Did you have a comfortable journey?' he enquired in a blandly matter-of-fact tone. 'Thank you, just leave the cases,' he added to the bell-boy, handing him a discreet tip. He leaned out into the corridor and caught Alysha under the elbow, drawing her into the room. 'Don't stand out there, darling,' he taunted, a lilt of sardonic humour in his voice. 'Come on in and tell me how much you've missed me.'

Before she had had time to realise fully what was happening, she was in his arms, and his mouth had closed over hers, sweetly demanding. She found herself responding helplessly, the past few weeks of lonely silence obliterated from her mind. It was as if they were back on their paradise island, with not much else to do but make love...

But as he swept her up in his arms and strode across the room with her towards the bedroom, reality returned with a jolt, and with it came anger. 'Hey!' she protested sharply. 'What do you think you're doing?'

He chuckled with laughter. 'You must have a very short memory if you have to ask that,' he teased.

'Put me down,' she insisted. 'What are you doing in my room?'

'*Our* room,' he corrected her mockingly, setting her on her feet. 'I booked in an hour ago—I came here straight from New York.'

'Oh—and just like that you expect me to fall into bed with you again?' she demanded, her fine eyes flashing in indignation. 'Well, I'm afraid you can just think again, Mr Elliot.'

She turned him an aloof shoulder, but as she put out her hand to open the door he reached over her shoulder, holding it firmly shut. 'Where are you going?' he taunted.

'To get myself another room.'

'They're full. Every hotel in town is fully booked for the collections.'

'I'll find somewhere,' she retorted with icy dignity.

He was still leaning one hand against the door, and as she gazed up at him in wary apprehension he put the other one up, effectively trapping her between his arms. He was in his customary denim shirt, and in the shadow of the open collar she could glimpse a few of those dark, rough curls that covered his chest. And with every breath the warm, male muskiness of his skin was drugging her mind...

'I'm...not going to let you treat me like this,' she insisted, her voice wavering.

'Like what?' he growled, his voice low and husky. 'Like this?' He bent his head, unerringly finding that sensitive spot in the hollow of her throat where her fluttering pulses raced, swirling the hot tip of his tongue over it in slow, languorous circles.

She shook her head, struggling to suppress the helpless tide of response that was rising inside her. 'Everyone will know—you know how they talk...'

'Let them,' he insisted ruthlessly, sliding his hands inside the folds of her warm trench-coat, and around her waist beneath her pink cashmere sweater, caressing her bare skin as his hard teeth nibbled erotically at the lobe of her ear. 'I haven't been able to get you out of my mind. All the time I've been away I've been thinking about you, thinking about your soft, warm skin, your glorious hair... It's been driving me half crazy...'

He knew far too well how to undermine her defences; his mouth was brushing across her face, dusting feather-light kisses across her trembling eyelids, the line of her cheekbone, sending hot little shivers scudding through her. His hand was caressing the curve of her spine, moulding her intimately close against him.

He was coaxing her inexorably across the room, until she felt the satin quilt of the bed behind her knees; and then she was tumbling back on to it as he fell with her, trapping her beneath him, his soft laughter mocking her inability to resist him.

Where the hell was her self-respect? she reproached herself bitterly. She hadn't even taken her coat off yet, for goodness' sake, and already he had pushed her sweater up to her throat, and the dainty lace scrap of her bra with it, exposing all the firm, naked swell of her breasts. His hands were caressing them, arousing them with an exquisite sensitivity, crushing them beneath his palms, and her tender nipples had hardened to ripe buds under that swirling abrasion, sending crackling sparks along her nerve fibres and into her brain.

She moaned softly, all the aching need of the past five weeks knotting inside her. He returned to claim her mouth again, parting her lips in hungry demand to plunder the sweet depths within, exploring with a flagrant sensuality, igniting all the familiar fires inside her.

His expert caresses were playing havoc with her senses; he knew just how to touch her, his fingertips trailing lazily over the aching swell of her breasts, tantalisingly skirting the rose-pink circles of her nipples until she was writhing beneath the exquisite torment.

He laughed down at her teasingly, and bent his head to blow a cool draught of air over the ripe buds, making her shiver with delight. And then he stretched out his tongue, lapping at each in turn, swirling around them as if they were ripe, succulent cherries, nipping at them gently with his hard white teeth, making her gasp in pleasure.

An urgent hunger was burning inside her, and she reached for him, needing desperately to feel his hot male flesh against hers. The buttons of his shirt seemed too complicated for her impatient fingers, and she ripped at them heedlessly, dragging them apart.

It felt so good to run her hands over that hard-muscled chest, to trail a path with her fingertips through the curling pelt of dark hair, to wrap her arms around him and arch her body beneath him, glorying in the delicious contrast between his fierce male power and her pliant feminine submissiveness.

With a swift tug he pulled the hem of her elegantly tailored skirt up around her waist, and ran his hands down over her slender thighs—making an interesting discovery. 'Stockings,' he approved, his voice a husky growl. 'Silk stockings. Perfect...'

A shiver of delight ran through her as his fingertips stroked lightly over the few inches of bare skin exposed above her stocking-tops, teasingly snapping at her suspenders; and then his hand slipped up to intrude beneath the silk and lace of the delicate French knickers she was wearing.

'More silk,' he murmured smokily. 'And in here—velvet.'

He was seeking the most intimate caresses, his clever fingers sliding into those moist, tender folds to explore and arouse, stroking gently over the tiny, exquisitely sensitive seed-pearl hidden within, and then thrusting deep inside her, making her gasp as the fierce shock of pleasure shafted through her.

His mouth was like fire as it trailed down the long, vulnerable curve of her throat and over her ripe, naked breasts, idly teasing her throbbing nipples with his languorous tongue, nipping at them, and finally taking one into his mouth to suckle at it with a fierce, pulsing rhythm that surged through her blood like a fever.

'What weren't you going to let me do to you?' he mocked softly, a glint of triumph in his eyes.

She shook her head, struggling to deny the ease with which she had let him seduce her again. 'You . . .'

He laughed as he slid off her French knickers, tossing them casually aside. They caught on the gilded wooden bed-post—a humiliating reminder of Gemma's prophetic words. How right she had been—one snap of his fingers, and she had become just one more in that long line of foolish females who had fallen victim to his beguiling snare.

But oh, it felt so good . . . As his hand slid up between her slender thighs she yielded in instinctive submission, her whole body awash with sweet sensations, her mind dissolving in the rapturous arousal of her senses. Her skin was incandescent with heat, all the more acutely felt because only parts of her were naked, the rest still clothed—as was Ross. The novelty of it, after the almost casual nudity of their days on the island, added an element of spice that proved her final downfall.

He rose to his feet, his hands going to the snap of his jeans, his eyes glinting with arrogant male pride as they slid down over her soft naked curves, savouring the erotic invitation as she lay back across the antique bed, her hair tumbled around her shoulders like a sable cloud, her breasts firm and ripe, tipped with succulent pink berries, her silk-clad thighs spread wide apart, the vulnerable cleft of crimson velvet beneath its crown of dusky curls offered to him in helpless surrender.

'So infinitely desirable,' he gloated on a husky growl. 'A sexy little plaything, as wanton as I could wish. Do you know how many times I've pictured you in my imagination, exactly like this? It's a miracle I've been able to get any business done at all.'

At least he hadn't forgotten her—even if his thoughts of her had been related solely to sex. But if that was the only part she could have in his life, it would have to be enough—like an addict, her need was stronger than her self-respect. As he came back down to her she reached up and wrapped her arms around him, submitting willingly to the deep, hard thrust as he took her.

It was as if they had never been apart. Their bodies moved to the same driving rhythm, an erotic dance as old as Adam and Eve. The friction of clothing against naked skin heightened the sweet intensity of sensation—was that why he had deliberately not undressed her? Or had it simply been the urgent frenzy of desire, fuelled by those frustrating weeks of separation?

The world had closed in around them like a dark velvet cloak, until there were only the two of them, and this moment of pure sensation. She could hear nothing but the sound of her own ragged breathing, the blood swirling through her veins. She was spinning in a vortex of mindless abandon, her body pliant beneath his fierce onslaught, striving to meet the full measure of his demand.

The strength of her own response almost shocked her; it was raw and primitive, stripped of all restraint. She was crying out, her spine arching in ecstasy, the bed bouncing violently beneath her. And then with a last wild surge the heat inside her exploded into flames, sweeping her up to dizzying heights, to let her fall at last, drifting in the swirling eddies, wrapped up in Ross's arms.

It was a long time before either of them moved. At last Alysha opened her eyes, gazing around at the room, enchanted by its discreet, old-fashioned elegance. The bed, like the rest of the furniture, was from the French Empire period, the serpentine headboard of carved and gilded rosewood padded with the same soft rose-pink damask that hung at the tall windows; the high ceiling was decorated with a tracery of plaster garlands, and from the centre of it hung an elaborate brass and crystal chandelier.

And there on the scrolled bedpost dangled her dainty white knickers, where Ross had discarded them so casually. With a stab of embarrassment at the wantonness of her own behaviour, she reached for them, slipped them back on as she rose to her feet and straightened the rest of her clothing.

Ross rolled over on to his back, resting against the pillows, his hands folded behind his head, watching as she wandered over to look out of the window at the view across the jumble of steeply pitched roofs of Paris to the romantic outline of the Eiffel Tower, silhouetted against the hazy blue of the winter sky.

'Changed your mind about finding another hotel?' he teased provocatively.

She turned back to him with a wry shrug. 'I suppose there isn't really much point,' she conceded, a careful nonchalance in her tone. 'You might at least have given me time to take my coat off first.'

He laughed, a gleam of wicked humour in his eyes. 'Impatience,' he excused himself insouciantly. 'You might have given me time to take my shirt off.'

She blushed vividly at the realisation that in her haste she had torn off several of his buttons. 'Oh!

I'm . . . sorry,' she stumbled. 'I'll . . . sew them back on for you.'

'It doesn't matter,' he assured her with casual unconcern. 'I've plenty more shirts.' He glanced at his watch. 'I've a meeting at two, but I've time for some lunch. There's a nice little bistro just around the corner. Fancy trying it?'

'Yes, fine.' She had been taking off her coat, but put it back on again. 'How was America?' she enquired, keeping her tone light, determined to turn the past few bleak weeks into a topic of light conversation to hide the pain she had felt that he hadn't even bothered with a phone call.

'Hectic,' he responded succinctly. 'What do you think—the green sweater or the navy?' He held up the two options to show her.

'The green one,' she chose, trying not to let herself take too much pleasure in the casual intimacy of the moment—it would be far too easy to get used to it.

CHAPTER NINE

THE wedding dress was stunning, a fantasy of shimmering white silk tulle straight out of *Gone With The Wind*. The tightly boned bodice had a daringly low off-the-shoulder neckline, trimmed with ruffles and white silk rosebuds, and was cinched in at her tiny waist with a ribbon sash; and then the skirt flounced out over a wide crinoline, caught up with more posies of rosebuds, the hemline sweeping the ground. The whole thing was completed by a parasol of the same white tulle, trimmed with the same pretty silk rosebuds.

Backstage at the *haute couture* shows was always pandemonium. Alysha did her best to ignore it as she scrambled into the priceless creation; half-naked models bickering over who was spreading herself over more than her fair share of space, hairdressers flitting around with canisters of hairspray adding frantic last minute touches to a fringe here, a ringlet there, dressers snarling at each other over missing pincushions and muddled shoes.

'Alysha, darling! Quickly, quickly!' Alain, the chubby, balding designer whose genius was responsible for all these fabulous creations, descended on her in a swoop, snatching the posy of pink silk roses that the dresser was about to pin to her corsage and tossing it aside. 'No no, it is too much!' he declared—though he himself had spent half an hour at the final fitting session agonising over that exact detail. 'It must be all white—pure and virginal.'

One of the other girls, dashing for the catwalk, sniggered as she passed. 'That's not what I heard,' she remarked loudly. 'With Ross Elliot for a room-mate?'

Alysha simply pretended not to have heard the comment; there had been plenty in a similar vein over the past two weeks. She had just had to accept that there was nothing she could do to stop the gossip and occasional bitchiness—it was part of the price she had to pay for these blissful happy days and nights with Ross. Besides, it would be wise not to say too much; by next season, she would be one of the discarded ones—someone else would be warming his bed.

And anyway, it was time for her entrance. The dresser handed her her shoes, and pausing only to spit swiftly on the soles to make them a little less slippery on the highly polished catwalk, she darted up the steps and stood waiting behind the wing-curtains, taking a few deep breaths to steady the flow of adrenalin that was racing through her veins.

The wedding-dress was the traditional grand finale of every show, and as it was announced and she stepped out into the dazzle of lights, coquettishly twirling her parasol, there was a ripple of approval that broke spontaneously into applause.

The room was hot beneath the glaring banks of television lights overhead, but she barely noticed; she barely heard the strains of the music either, nor saw the ranks of upturned faces crowded around the raised catwalk—every important fashion editor and buyer from all over the world, as well as the aristocrats and billionaires' wives and Hollywood princesses who were among the privileged few who could afford the kind of prices Alain could command for one of his fantastic creations.

Selecting at random one vaguely familiar face—
hadn't she recently won an Oscar or something?—she
moved forward, a smooth glide that made her seem
to float on air. Halfway along the catwalk she turned,
and paused while the photographers crowded in, their
lenses like great black saucer-eyes, unblinking. And
then on, right to the end of the catwalk, turning again
before gliding back to the curtains to pose one last
time.

Ross was out there somewhere. He had had to go
back to London for a couple of days, but he had returned last night, very late, creeping into bed when
she was already asleep and waking her by making love
to her. It seemed a little ironic that he should be
standing out there in the shadows, watching her model
a wedding gown; it was unlikely that she would ever
wear one for him.

And then it was all over. The audience had burst
into wild applause, calling for Alain, and he came out
to take his bow, his cherubic face flushed with delight
and relief—the tension he had been under for the past
few weeks must have been tremendous. Taking
Alysha's hand, and on the other side one of the other
girls, he stepped forward and bowed again, and then
blowing kisses to his adoring admirers he skipped back
through the curtains and collapsed into a flimsy plastic
chair.

'Champagne!' he gasped theatrically. 'I am going
to faint!'

He didn't, of course. As the applause died away
and the crowds out front began to disperse, the tension
backstage uncoiled into elation. A favoured few from
among the audience—and those who thought they
should be among the favoured few—were clustering
around to congratulate the maestro. Alysha found

herself trapped in the middle of the mob, still wearing the wedding-dress.

'Darling—it's just *exquisite*,' shrieked one elderly dowager of substantial proportions. 'It made me wish I could be a bride again. Not that I could ever look as adorable in it as you do, my dear,' she added gushingly to Alysha. 'It's absolute perfection on you.'

'Thank you,' Alysha murmured a little self-consciously. She was longing to get away, to get out of this damned dress; Ross had just come in, and was standing not five feet away from her, chatting to one of the people from Italian *Vogue*—the last thing she wanted was for him to think that she was keeping the dress on deliberately, that it was giving her some sort of stupid romantic ideas. He would run a mile.

But there was no way she could escape the limelight. Alain had leapt to his feet, catching both her hands and lifting them to his lips in a gesture of extravagant gallantry. 'That is right exactly!' he declared. 'Absolute perfection! I shall not sell it—this would be sacrilege. I shall save it for you to wear on your wedding-day! It shall be my present for you!'

Her mouth twitched into a nervous smile. From the corner of her eye she could see Ross, watching the scene, a glint of enigmatic humour in those hard grey eyes—he must certainly have heard what Alain had said. Laughing merrily, she shook her head. 'Oh, Alain, don't be so old-fashioned! Who gets married these days?'

The portly *couturier* pouted, but then he slanted a covert glance towards Ross, and a gleam of comprehension lit his eyes. 'All right,' he whispered, winking at her mischievously. 'But all the same, I think I shall just put it away for a little while, and see what happens, eh?'

Her soft mouth quirked into a wry smile. 'I'm afraid it would be a terrible waste, Alain,' she responded quietly. 'I very much doubt if I should ever get to wear it.'

He patted her hand. 'Well, never mind. I shan't sell it anyway—to be honest, on almost anyone else but you it would look a complete fright.'

At last the throng was beginning to disperse, some of them to catch the next show, others to head back to Alain's studio on the Rue Bonaparte, where a sumptuous buffet lunch awaited them. Alysha glanced around for the dresser to help her out of the elaborate gown, but she seemed to have vanished along with everyone else...

'That's quite a dress.' Ross was at her side, a faintly sardonic smile curving that hard, sensual mouth as he subjected her to a mocking appraisal.

She shrugged her slender shoulders in a gesture of casual indifference. 'You think so?' she responded lightly, determined to dispel any suspicion that she might have let herself get caught up in the fairy-tale. 'I think it's a little over the top myself.'

He lifted one dark eyebrow in quizzical amusement. 'But then, doesn't every girl dream of a dress that's a little over the top on her wedding-day?' he enquired.

She laughed merrily, shaking her head. 'Not these days,' she asserted. 'Most of us are far too busy building up our careers to have any time for that sort of romantic nonsense... I wonder where Adèle has got to?' she added, changing the subject before it got dangerous. 'I need to get out of this dress.'

'I can help you.'

The husky note in his voice brought a tinge of pink to her cheeks. They were alone now—everyone else had gone. 'Oh... No, it's...all right, thank you,' she assured him quickly. 'I can manage.'

He slanted a sardonic glance down at the back of the dress, with its long row of tiny hand-made silk buttons. 'I think you'll need a hand,' he insisted in a voice of lazy mockery. 'Unless you're a contortionist.'

He didn't wait for her to argue, but turned her firmly around, and began to unfasten the buttons, one by one. The brush of his fingers against her warm skin sent a hot little shiver through her—it was incredible the way that every time he touched her he could still set her pulses racing as swiftly as if it had been the very first time.

The tight basque began to fall loose as he unfastened the buttons, and she hugged it up over her breasts in instinctive defensiveness—beneath it, all she had on was the tiny white lace G-string which was the most practical thing to wear when she had to jump in and out of fifteen different outfits, with little more than half a minute for each change, and any visible line would have been a disaster.

He sensed her response, laughing softly. 'What's wrong?' he taunted. 'You don't usually mind me undressing you.'

'I...I know,' she stammered, 'but...someone might come in...'

'They've all gone to lunch.' He stroked his hands over her bare shoulders, drawing her back against him and bending his head into the sensitive hollow below her ear, swirling it with the hot tip of his tongue.

'Careful,' she protested, her voice unsteady. 'You're...crushing the dress.'

'Then take it off.'

'I ought to wait for Adèle...'

He slid his hands inside the dress, stroking them caressingly over the peach-smooth curve of her stomach. 'I can't believe how much you make me want you,' he growled, his breath warm in her hair. 'I can never get enough of you.'

'Ross, don't!' she protested breathlessly, trying to pull away from him. 'Not in here—not now . . .'

His only response was that husky laughter, as he slipped his hands up beneath hers to mould the ripe curve of her aching breasts, teasing the tender nipples into a state of exquisite arousal. Her head tipped back against his shoulder, and his mouth closed over hers in melting seduction, his tongue swirling languorously into all the sweetest depths within.

'Take the dress off,' he coaxed in husky urgency.

She could only do as he bid, stepping out of it carefully, her shocked eyes catching sight of her virtually naked body in the mirrors that lined the room as he drew her inexorably into his arms, the rough texture of his denim jeans and cashmere sweater rasping deliciously against her heated skin.

'We really shouldn't be doing this,' she argued weakly.

'That's what makes it too tempting to resist,' he growled, easing her back against the long shelf that ran along beneath the row of mirrors where a short while ago the make-up team had been so busy. Perching her up on the edge of it, he slid his hands down over the soft curves of her body, deftly slipping the tiny lace G-string down over her slender thighs and letting it fall to the floor.

His strong thighs nudged hers insistently apart, and she could only surrender as he unsnaped his jeans and drew her in to meet the hard thrust as he took her. All around them, the mirrors reflected back the scene

from every angle—the gleaming honey-gold of her
naked body in his arms, her slender legs wrapped
around him, the powerful, rhythmic pounding as he
took his urgent pleasure.

She drew in a ragged breath, her head tipping back,
her eyes closed. This was crazy—why was she letting
him do it to her? Someone could come along at any
moment . . . But she knew why she was letting him do
it; because she wanted him every bit as much as he
wanted her, because when he touched her she didn't
know how to resist him—and because if she was absolutely honest the sheer wantonness of it, the danger
of getting caught, added a spice that ignited her senses,
inflaming her responses to white heat.

This was no gentle lovemaking—there was no time.
It was swift and feverish, peaking on a fierce wave of
pleasure that left her weak and breathless—if Ross
hadn't been holding her up, she would have slid to
the floor.

He laughed in husky satisfaction, his breath warm
in her hair. 'That was incredible,' he murmured
smokily. 'Every time I make love to you, I want you
more. I want you to move into my house, to be there
every night, in my bed—to live with me.'

Her heart kicked so hard against her ribs that she
was sure he must have heard it. Move in with him—
live with him? Oh, yes . . . Oh, no! she dared not let
herself be lured down that primrose path; it could lead
only to disaster. Forcing a merry laugh, she shook her
head.

'You mean give up my own flat? Don't be silly. Besides, how can I be there every night? You've got me
lined up for trips all over the place—I've got to go to
New York next Tuesday, and I'll only be back just in
time for the Milan collections, and then it's off to

California and Hawaii before I've hardly even had time to touch down.'

'All the more reason why we should live together,' he argued persuasively. 'I have to be away on business a lot too—why not arrange it so that the time we *do* have we can be together?'

Oh, it was so tempting. But, as with his invitation to spend Christmas with him in Australia, he had made it all too painfully clear that he was thinking only of the convenience of being able to make love to her whenever he felt like it—he was offering not a particle of romance, of commitment, of love. And if she were to accept, she would be giving up every-thing—her independence, her self-respect; and when it ended, she would be left with nothing.

Firmly shaking her head again, she moved away from him before his beguiling caresses could undermine her will. Crossing the room, she picked up her tote-bag from beneath the chair where she had left it, unzipping it and pulling out her clothes.

'No—I really don't think it would be a good idea,' she insisted, the lightness of her tone concealing the turmoil of her emotions. She felt a little better as she slipped into her underwear and shrugged a soft rose-pink silk shirt over her shoulders, focusing all her at-tention on fastening the buttons. 'I told you before, I want to concentrate on my career at the moment.'

'That's fine by me,' he countered, coming over to stand close behind her as she stopped to peer into the low run of mirror fixed to the wall, carefully creaming the thick layer of stage make-up from her face. A hint of impatience was creeping into his voice. 'I've no intention of interfering with your career—I'm the one you're under contract to, remember?'

'I know. But it always seems to happen. It's a funny thing, but it's always the woman who seems to sacrifice the most in a relationship, and the man who gets all the benefits. I don't want to spend my life ironing your shirts and washing your socks...'

'I've a housekeeper to do that, for goodness' sake...!'

But before he could argue further the door flew open, and the dresser bustled into the room. 'Ah, *chérie*—I am so sorry! I went to see that the van was here to transport the clothes back to the salon.' She glanced at the discarded dress, and then at Ross, her eyes glinting with a very French understanding of exactly what had been going on. 'But you have managed without me, hmm?'

Ross smiled with wry humour, casually picking up the betraying evidence of Alysha's white G-string from the floor and dropping it into her bag. She blushed scarlet, scrambling swiftly into her clothes, grateful at least that the dresser hadn't returned a few moments earlier.

With a gesture of mocking gallantry, Ross held her coat for her, enfolding her in his arms as he wrapped it around her shoulders. 'All right—if that's the way you want it,' he acknowledged in what she suspected would prove only a temporary concession. 'Come on—let's go and grab some lunch while there's still some left.'

The flickering firelight danced on the walls and ceiling. Alysha sighed luxuriously, and stretched out on the kelim rug, wriggling her toes in front of the flames. 'Mmm—there's nothing to beat lying in front of a real fire.'

'There's nothing to beat lying in front of a real fire with a beautiful woman,' Ross amended. 'Especially when she's naked.' He ran his hand up over the peach-smooth curve of her stomach and settled it beneath the firm swell of her breasts in a comfortably intimate gesture.

Alysha laughed, twisting her head to smile teasingly up at him—he was naked too, lying at an angle to her across the rug, her head nestled on his shoulder. 'I never seem to keep my clothes on very long when I come here,' she remarked.

'I know.' His thumb was brushing lightly, almost absently, over the taut nub of her nipple. 'Sometimes I think you're just using me for sex.'

'Of course,' she retorted mischievously. 'And don't you just love it?'

'Oh, I'm not complaining,' he groaned with husky sensuality, lifting himself up on one elbow to concentrate more intently on his task. 'What beats me is why you won't just move in with me. What possible harm could it do to your career, for goodness' sake? I don't want to stop you working—you can go on modelling for as long as you like.'

Oh, it would have been so easy to let herself be persuaded! But she had to hold on to her independence at all costs—otherwise, when the affair came to its inevitable end, she would be left with nothing at all. So she shook her head.

'But I don't just want to do modelling,' she insisted. 'I've only got a few more years at the top, anyway. Then I want to try to get into television. That's going to take a lot of hard work—I have to give it all my attention.'

'At the expense of everything else?'

'If necessary.'

With a sigh of angry impatience, he lay back on the rug, his hands folded beneath his head, clearly signalling that he didn't want to touch her. 'You really are the most damned obstinate woman I've ever met!' he snapped testily. 'You're in danger of letting your precious career become an obsession.'

Alysha peeped up at him from beneath her lashes, torn between her own longing to do as he wanted and her fear of letting herself become submerged in the relationship. It was bad enough already—it was only six weeks since Paris, and already she found it impossible to remember what life had been like without him.

They hadn't even been together a great deal. She had been very busy—there had been the Milan *couture* shows, and several trips to America on promotional tours for Lozier, as well as working in the studios to complete the television commercials.

And Ross had been away for much of the time too. She had been a little startled to learn how extensive his business interests were; she had thought there was only the London-based advertising agency that she already knew about. But it seemed that he owned substantial slices of similar agencies in Europe, America and the Far East, as well as a publishing company in Australia and a well-known chain of high street photographic shops.

Most of the time they could snatch to be together they spent making love; after panicking for a second time after Paris that she might be pregnant, Alysha had now been careful to take the appropriate precautions—though not without the occasional wistful twinge of longing for the baby she dared not risk allowing herself to have.

But there had been time for talking too, and in the soft afterglow of their lovemaking he had sometimes let down his guard a little. And the more she had learned about him, the more deeply she had fallen in love with him—his character had turned out to be far more complex and interesting than she had believed.

This house, for instance—it wasn't at all what she had been expecting. She had placed him in a modern city flat, full of slick furniture and jazzy gadgets; instead he lived in a tall, old-fashioned house high on a leafy hill overlooking Greenwich Park, with a long, narrow, walled garden full of fruit trees, and this spacious book-lined sitting-room, with its real coal fire burning, and its comfortable chesterfield sofas. The gadgets were there—a state-of-the-art hi-fi system, a wide-format television with video recorders and attachment to the cable network—but they blended into rather than dominated the room.

And as she had learned more about his background, she had come to understand what drove him. Brought up by an aunt who didn't seem to have been particularly enthusiastic about him, he had rebelled against her, against school, against just about everything—until an early brush with the law had put him on an alternative education scheme, where someone had put a camera in his hands, and he had seen a way of escaping the dismal destiny that had seemed to be mapped out for him.

And now, at the age of thirty-five, he seemed to have reached all the goals he had set for himself—or at least to be well on his way. And would that prove to be enough for him? Or would he, perhaps, one day begin to want just one woman to share his life with, a child to whom he could pass on the fruits of all his energy...?

Maybe. And maybe—just maybe—if she could play the game well enough, if she could make him always want just that little bit more than she was giving, if she could avoid the fatal trap of letting him see how much she loved him, of doing or saying something that he might perceive as making demands on him, she might be able to hold on long enough to be in the right place at the right time when he began to feel that need. Maybe.

But how long *could* she hold on? Three months— that was usually about as long as his affairs lasted. And if you counted just from Paris, she was already halfway through. If you counted from Thailand, there was very little time left . . .

Tentatively she reached out her hand to touch him. He didn't respond, but he didn't push her away either—and he had accused her of being obstinate! But he had taught her well over these past six weeks, and though she had been a willing pupil, it wasn't only his instruction that had educated her—her own imagination, fired by instincts as old as Eve, had played its part as well. His indifference was a challenge to her newly acquired skills.

Slowly she let her fingertips trail through that feral pelt of rough, dark hair across his wide chest. His skin was bronzed a few shades darker than her own, warm over the resilient spring of muscle, and its scent had an evocative male muskiness that stirred her senses on a level far too deep for rational thought.

If her three months were almost up, there might not be any more nights like this; and if that was to be the case she was determined that he would remember her among all the others—she would give him just that little bit more pleasure, that would make her harder to forget.

Kneeling across him, the soft amber glow of the fire dancing over her naked body, she smiled down at him in bewitching promise—though the hard glint in those steel-grey eyes warned her that he was in no mood to co-operate.

She bent over him, letting the silken fall of her hair stroke against his skin as she dusted delicate kisses along the hard line of his collarbone, finding the spot where his strong pulse beat in the hollow of his throat and swirling it languorously with her tongue, and then trailing up to nibble lightly at the lobe of his ear.

He couldn't suppress the tremor of response that ran through him, and she chuckled in delight, intoxicated by this new-found power. 'You can get as angry as you like,' she taunted, daringly provocative. 'I know just how to turn you to putty.'

Very slowly, deliberately tormenting him, she began to move down, digressing to visit a number of places she knew could produce a very interesting reaction. But they both knew her objective, and she slanted him a wickedly seductive glance as she reached it.

'Well, maybe not *putty*,' she amended in husky appreciation, stroking one finger along his impressive male hardness.

It was the tender intimacy of this act she loved. Her soft mouth and delicate hands were weaving their witchcraft on him, teasing and tantalising him, torturing him with pleasure. In most of their lovemaking he was the active one, while she had only to respond; but in this she could take the initiative, be creative— do things that would once have shocked her even to think about.

And there was no mistaking how much he enjoyed it; his breathing was ragged, and he groaned as if in agony, powerful tremors shuddering through him. He put down his hand to caress her hair gently, and she peeped up from beneath her lashes to see his face, to see the shadows of pleasure dancing over it.

Usually at this point she would stop, and they would make love in a more conventional way; but this time she didn't want to stop—she wanted to finish what she had started. 'Alysha?' he queried on a note of surprise, but the spark of sinful intent in her eyes answered him.

A small thrill—a compound of excitement and apprehension—ran through her. He was rapidly approaching the peak of his arousal, his muscles clenching and his spine rigid; all the love she couldn't speak aloud was concentrated on giving him the most exquisite moment of ecstasy. And then with a hot surge the tension inside him exploded, recoiling like a small earthquake, leaving that magnificent body for a short time weak and helpless.

Alysha laughed in gentle teasing, sliding up into his arms. 'You see? Why risk spoiling what we've got by being greedy? We enjoy the time we have together all the more *because* it's limited—we both have other interests, and we don't have time to get bored with each other. It's the perfect arrangement.'

He slanted her a somewhat crooked smile. 'All right, you've made your point,' he conceded reluctantly. 'That was . . . pretty good.'

CHAPTER TEN

'IT'S snowing.' Alysha shivered, and let the curtain fall back over the window. 'I'd better be going.'

'Why?' Ross demanded, an edge of annoyance in his voice. 'You could stay the night, you know—you'd be more than welcome.'

'I stayed last night,' she reminded him, shaking her head. 'We agreed—the odd night is OK, but not more than that.'

'What's wrong with the odd *two* nights?' he countered abrasively. 'The world wouldn't come to an end, you know.'

She sighed, glancing round at the cosy room, softly bathed in the flickering glow of the firelight. It was so warm and cosy in here—and so cold outside. Would there really be any harm in staying, just this one night? But she knew that there would. It would be the thin end of the wedge—soon two nights would lead to 'Why not three?' and before she knew it she would have more of her things here than at her own place.

'Please—we've discussed it so many times,' she insisted with quiet determination. 'I don't want to argue about it again.'

Ross uttered a fierce oath under his breath, sitting up and dragging on his jeans. 'All right—if you prefer to go out on a filthy night like this, when you could be tucked up in a warm bed with me, you'd better go home,' he grated. 'What about tomorrow night? Can you spare me a little of your precious time?'

She shook her head. 'I'm...going home for the weekend,' she explained a little awkwardly. She hadn't actually told him about her father yet, nor about the reduced circumstances in which her family now lived; he had been attracted to a certain image of her, and she was afraid to risk shattering that fragile illusion—what if he wasn't interested in the real her?

Those steel-grey eyes had hardened. 'Going home again?' he queried. 'It's only two weeks since the last time you went.'

'I know,' she countered defensively. 'But they... expect it.'

'All right,' he grated. 'I'll come with you.'

She stared up at him, startled. 'What?'

He laughed in cold humour. 'What's wrong? Afraid I'll show you up by saying settee instead of sofa, or holding my knife the wrong way?'

'No... Of course not. It's just...'

'That's the bottom line, isn't it?' he remarked, his voice laced with harsh cynicism. 'It's got nothing to do with your damned precious career. I just don't have the requisite breeding—I'm a mongrel from the rough end of Glasgow, who still prefers watching Spurs to going to the ballet, and would rather drink a good pint of bitter than a glass of fancy claret. Basically, my dear, we don't have a lot in common—maybe we should just call it a day.'

Her heart thudded, and seemed to stop. 'Call it a day?' she whispered, hurt and bewildered. 'What do you mean?'

'It sounded like pretty plain English to me,' he countered caustically. 'It's over, finished, ended—you and I have an ex-relationship. Is that clear enough for you?'

It was—devastatingly clear. Alysha dragged in a ragged breath, struggling to retain some semblance of dignity. It was such a stupid quarrel—they had been through it so many times before. Why suddenly this extreme reaction? Or was it just an excuse, a way of engineering a break-up while laying the blame on her?

Hot tears were prickling the backs of her eyes, but she refused to shed them—she had promised herself from the beginning that when the time came she would at least walk away with some dignity. Tilting up her chin, she met his eyes levelly.

'All right,' she conceded, her voice commendably even. 'If that's the way you want it. I . . . just have a few things here—I'd better go and fetch them. I won't be a moment.'

Somehow she managed to get out of the room, though her legs were trembling so much she felt as if she was going to collapse. But she had to get away before the dangerous weakness that was threatening to engulf her had her collapsing in tears at his feet, begging him to give her one more night, one more week.

The stairs were like a mountain. Opening the door to his bedroom, she had to avert her eyes from the massive double bed, with its thick hand-woven wool coverlet—there were just too many memories . . .

How on earth had she managed to accumulate so many things here in so short a time? There were three pairs of earrings, a pair of shoes, a pink lambswool sweater . . . each an achingly poignant reminder of a cosy dinner in front of the fire, a midnight walk in the park. But she wanted no excuse to come back, so she gathered them all up quickly and hurried back down the stairs.

Ross was in the sitting-room, standing at the window, gazing out at the falling snow. He glanced back over his shoulder as she hesitated in the doorway, that hard-boned face giving away nothing of what he was thinking. He glanced at the bundle in her arms, one dark eyebrow lifting in sardonic enquiry. 'Sure you've got everything?'

She returned him a frosty glare. 'Not quite,' she enunciated tautly. 'I want . . . the pictures.'

'Which pictures?' But he knew perfectly well.

'The ones you took on the island,' she insisted. 'And . . . the ones from before.'

'I've already told you I'm not going to publish them,' he responded, a note of taunting mockery in his voice. 'Don't you trust me?'

She returned him a cold glare—she had nothing left to lose anyway. 'No, I don't.'

Just for one brief moment those cool grey eyes betrayed a searing heat of anger, but then he shrugged his wide shoulders in a gesture of hardened indifference. 'Then I'll get them for you,' he conceded drily.

He took the stairs two at a time, up to his attic studio and dark-room. A moment later she heard him return, a grey box-file in his hands. 'There. I think you'll find everything is in there,' he drawled in a tone of casual dismissal. 'Polaroids, contacts, negatives. Satisfied?'

'Yes. Thank you,' she mumbled. She felt as if she was slowly sliding into a deep black pit of despair, but she was still determined to put a brave face on it, so she forced herself to meet his flinty gaze. 'Well I . . . I'll see you around then, I suppose . . .'

'Probably,' he confirmed drily. 'I've no intention of releasing you from your contract.'

'I . . . wasn't expecting you to.' Drawing in a deep, steadying breath, she held out her hand. 'Well . . . Goodbye, then.'

That hard mouth quirked into a humourless smile. 'Goodbye,' he responded, making no move to take her hand.

For one last moment she hesitated, searching those granite features for just some tiny hint that he might change his mind. But there was none. She had known that it would come to an end, of course, and probably sooner rather than later, but she hadn't expected it to be so . . . sudden. Part of her had even been stupid enough to believe that he was beginning to feel something for her.

Turning away from him, she opened the front door—he didn't help her, even though she had her hands full—and stepped into the softly falling snow. As she walked down the path, she heard the door close behind her.

The drifting flakes danced golden in the light of the street-lamps, and a fine covering of it lay over everything, not yet disturbed. It seemed to deaden every sound, so that it was easy to imagine in that quiet back street that she was the only person in the whole world who was out of doors. Lifting her face, she felt the wet flakes brush on to her cheeks, melting and mingling with the tears which were welling silently from her eyes.

Her mind was still grappling to catch up with what had happened. One moment she had been lying there, warm and safe in his arms; the next she was standing out here on his garden path in the snow, the fragile, tentative links that had been growing between them abruptly severed—cut off but still hurting like amputated nerve-fibres.

She stood there for a long time, as if caught in a kind of limbo—once she stepped off this path on to the public pavement, it really would be over, irrevocably. But she couldn't stay here all night in front of that closed door, as the snow fell around her—she would soon look like a snowman. If he would only open the door...

But it was no use waiting for that, she reminded herself bitterly—hell would freeze over first. Drawing on every ounce of willpower she possessed, she walked out to where her car was parked at the kerb.

'A *summons*?' Alysha frowned, taking the telephone over to the armchair and sitting down. 'What on earth have you got a summons for?'

'It's just a stupid little motoring offence,' Audrey Fordham-Jones declared loftily. 'It's a pity the police don't have anything better to do than going around harassing perfectly respectable motorists for every trivial little mistake.'

Alysha rolled her tawny eyes heavenwards in exasperation. 'What exactly did you do, Mother?' she enquired evenly.

'I simply reversed the car. I'd missed my exit from the motorway, and it would have been most inconvenient to have to carry on to the next one—it's more than six miles. It's not as if I hadn't pulled over on to the hard shoulder. And as for the police car, I didn't realise they were coming up behind me—I didn't do a great deal of damage to it, and I offered to pay at once. And as for the business about the insurance... Well, it was just ridiculous, the amount they were asking for! I refused to pay—and now the police are making a fuss about that, too.'

'Let me get this straight,' Alysha requested with careful patience. 'You were reversing on the motorway, you hit a police car, and you were driving without insurance? Is there anything else?'

'Of course not,' her mother countered indignantly. 'Except that I have to appear in court next Friday. I shall need you to come with me—I can't possibly go by myself, and I can't ask dear Oliver when he has these important exams coming up.'

Alysha pulled a wry face. 'Next Friday? I don't know—it's a bit difficult at such short notice. I'm supposed to be doing a fashion shoot for *Cosmopolitan.*'

'Well, surely you can put them off?' Audrey demanded in querulous tones. 'Heaven knows, I don't ask very much of you—I should have thought you could put yourself out just this once.'

Alysha sighed. 'All right, Mother—I'll do my best.'

Well, at least it was something to take her mind off her own misery, she reflected as she put the phone down. It had been nearly two weeks now; if time was supposed to be the great healer, it wasn't working very well—as the numbness was wearing off the pain was getting worse.

At least she hadn't had to endure the agony of meeting him—he was in America, on business. Maybe by the time he got back she would have recovered sufficiently to face him with a measure of equanimity. Maybe. Or maybe she would just crumble into tears, making a complete fool of herself.

But she daren't let herself dwell on thoughts of Ross. Resolutely she pushed them from her mind, and picked up the phone again, dialling the number of the Faces agency—she would need to speak to her booker about rearranging her schedule. What excuse could she give? Something urgent had cropped up at home; she would have to avoid giving details—it wasn't exactly the sort of thing she wanted bandied about.

The court building was a red-brick monstrosity in the middle of town, a tribute to the cut-price public architecture of the late twentieth century. Alysha managed to find a space for her white Metro in the multi-storey car park opposite, and they crossed the busy main road at the traffic lights.

That last flurry of winter snow in early March had given way to the first stirrings of spring; the sky was a pale, water-colour blue, the sun cool but bright, and the corporation flower beds in front of the court building were a mass of yellow daffodils.

But Alysha wasn't in the mood to appreciate any of it. She glanced around almost furtively as they reached the imposing entrance—the hairs on the back of her neck were prickling with the uncomfortable sensation that unseen eyes were watching her every move. Stupid, of course, she reassured herself sensibly—the Lozier campaign wasn't due to be launched for another couple of weeks, so she was still just a face in the crowd.

But nevertheless she couldn't shake the feeling. It haunted her as they checked the list pinned to the notice board to find out which court her mother's case was listed in, and as they sat at one of the utilitarian formica-topped tables in the smoke-filled canteen, cautiously sipping ditchwater coffee from polystyrene cups.

If only Audrey hadn't chosen to wear her mink, she reflected with a touch of asperity—it was probably that which was calling attention to them. She glanced around over her shoulder again, surveying the waiting area outside, but there was no one she even thought she recognised.

'I hope we won't be kept waiting much longer,' her mother declared, shuddering with distaste as a large youth with tattoos on his arms slid into the next table—the chairs were fixed to the floor, which made it a little awkward for anyone not of standard size to sit down. 'Ten o'clock, it said on the papers—quite clearly. We've been here for more than an hour already! Most inefficient, I call it.'

'Unfortunately we don't have any choice but to wait,' Alysha warned her patiently. 'You don't want them to issue a warrant for your arrest. Is your solicitor here yet?'

'Gerald? Yes, I saw him earlier, while you were queueing for the coffee. He promised to try to hurry it up a bit. Ah—there he is now. And he's waving us over. Perhaps they've *finally* decided to call us in.'

To Alysha's relief, that proved to be the case. She slipped into the back of the court, on the seats set aside for the public, watching anxiously as her mother stalked imperiously to the front, where defendants had to sit. If only she would have the sense to behave with a little appropriate humility, Alysha mused wryly. She just didn't seem to understand that she could make matters far worse for herself by appearing to treat the whole proceedings with such haughty disdain . . .

'Mind if I sit here?'

A sharp thud of shock almost took her breath away. 'Wh-what are you doing here?' she gasped in an agitated whisper. 'I thought you were in America!'

Ross smiled down at her, those deep-set grey eyes glinting with wry humour.

Alysha sat dumbstruck, hardly paying any attention to what was happening at the front of the court as the charges against her mother were read out and the lawyers debated the somewhat farcical incident in tones of heavy solemnity. She couldn't even begin to think straight—the whole world had turned upside down.

But she wasn't dreaming. The man beside her was real and solid; his hard shoulder was touching hers, and she was breathing that faint, familiar, musky scent that was exclusively his. How had he known she would be here? She hadn't told a soul, not even Bobbie— he hadn't even been due back from America until next week.

Whether it was five minutes or five hours that she sat there she had no idea—in fact it was about twenty minutes. The solicitors were gathering up their papers, and the next case was already being called as Audrey walked back down the court, wearing a somewhat chastened expression. Ross put his hand beneath Alysha's elbow and helped her to her feet.

'Come on,' he urged softly. 'Let's get out of here.'

She stumbled past the row of chairs and back out to the waiting area, her mind still a turmoil of confusion. Her mother had been detained by her solicitor for a few moments, and she turned to Ross in bewilderment.

'What are you doing here?' she demanded raggedly. 'When did you get back from America? How did you know where I was?'

He drew her back into a quiet corner, half hidden from the room by a large square pillar. 'Just a couple of hours ago,' he returned, an inflection of ironic self-mockery in his voice. 'I flew Concorde. I only heard yesterday that you'd pulled out of today's fashion shoot, on account of some unexplained "personal business"—and... Well, I'm afraid I jumped to what appears to have been the wrong conclusion. The reason I knew where to find you was that I've had a private detective watching you since six o'clock this morning—he followed you here, and reported back to me as soon as I landed.'

'But... why?' she queried, more puzzled than ever. 'I don't understand. What did you think I was doing?'

He drew her firmly into his arms, refusing to let her go. 'I thought you were going to have an abortion,' he responded grimly. 'I wasn't going to let you.'

'An *abortion*?' She realised with a sudden twinge of embarrassment that she had spoken too loudly, her voice echoing off the bare brick walls. 'What on earth gave you a crazy idea like that?' she added rather more discreetly.

'It didn't seem crazy at the time,' he confessed, a shadow passing behind those smoky eyes. 'We hadn't been taking precautions—it seemed like a pretty fair assumption that you were likely to get pregnant. I was waiting, hoping... It seemed like the one thing that might make a difference. But you never said anything. And then when I found out you'd pulled out of an important shoot... I knew it had to be something really serious.'

'But an *abortion*?' she protested. 'How could you think I'd even *dream* of doing something like that?'

'Well, a baby wouldn't exactly be a good career move right now, would it?' he countered bitterly. 'And your career's so damned important to you.'

'Not that damned important!' she retorted. 'Besides, I'm not stupid—I knew I was likely to get pregnant if we carried on seeing each other, so I went on the Pill as soon as we got back from Paris.'

He grinned crookedly. 'I suppose I should have guessed as much,' he conceded. 'If you weren't willing to risk your career by getting married, you certainly wouldn't have wanted a baby yet. And I wouldn't have expected you to—I would have been willing to wait for that. Was that what you were afraid of? Was that why you were so unwilling to commit yourself?'

'*I* was unwilling?' she protested, her head in a spin. 'How was I supposed to know that was what you wanted? You never told me—you made me think you were only interested in ... sex!'

His eyes sparked with wicked amusement. 'Well, I have to admit that was the main thing on my mind a lot of the time,' he confessed. 'But it was a lot more than that. From the first time I met you, you had an effect on me that I didn't understand—I thought you were just a stuck-up little bitch who'd come into my studio with a hundred pounds in her purse, just begging to be taken down a peg.'

'Well, yes ... I suppose I deserved it,' she conceded wryly. 'I behaved like a complete idiot.'

He shook his head. 'You were just young, and very naïve. What happened that afternoon haunted me for years. I thought it was just a guilty conscience for what I'd done, until you came back on to the modelling circuit, and I began to see your picture everywhere, hear people talking about you. I wanted to get in touch with you sooner, but...I kept finding reasons not to. Then when the Lozier contract came along— you were just so perfect for it, I realised I had to take the risk of seeing you again.'

She stared up at him, still half bewildered. 'Was it really so much of a risk?'

'It turned out to be a far greater risk than I'd been afraid of,' he admitted, that fascinating mouth curved into a wry smile. 'From the minute you walked into that restaurant I've been a lost cause.'

'Oh?' She slanted him a look of wary suspicion. 'What about Bobbie, then? Are you telling me you *weren't* having an affair with her?'

He laughed in gentle teasing. 'No, I wasn't. You were really determined to believe all the gossip about me, weren't you?'

'Well, you never denied it,' she pointed out with a touch of asperity.

'Would you have believed me?'

'Well . . . No,' she conceded.

'Exactly. Besides, I was doing a favour for Bobbie,' he added on a note of dry humour. 'She had her sights firmly set on Sir Richard, and she needed a plausible escort to help her play him on her line. And I was quite willing to oblige—partly as an old friend, and partly because you were treating me as if I had rabies.'

'And Gemma?' she queried, still unconvinced. 'Was that a favour for an old friend too?'

He shook his head. 'I did *not* sleep with Gemma in Bangkok—I don't know where you got the crazy idea from that I did. Quite apart from the fact that she was a mistake I had no intention of repeating, don't you know that once I'd met you again there was never going to be anyone else? In fact, once I'd met you for the first time there was never going to be anyone else,' he added huskily. 'Every woman I went out with I was unconsciously comparing with the sweet memory I carried inside my head—that's why none of them ever lasted very long.'

She gazed up into his eyes, at last beginning to let herself believe he might be telling the truth. 'And that's the very reason I was afraid of getting involved with you,' she whispered. 'You had such a reputation . . .'

'Most of it very much exaggerated,' he assured her. 'Oh, I don't pretend to have been a saint, but I haven't been quite the alley-cat I've been painted, either.'

'But... I really don't understand.' She frowned, still afraid to let herself take all this at face value. 'If that's so, why did you say the things you said that night? Why did you tell me it was all over?'

'Because I couldn't take any more—it was hurting too much. You just wouldn't let me get close. Maybe I was rushing you, trying to insist on you coming to live with me, but I was so much in love with you I couldn't wait. I was hoping that once we were actually living together, it wouldn't seem such a big step to you to go the whole hog and get married. But it seemed as though the harder I pushed you, the more you backed away,' he added, a raw note in his voice. 'I was experiencing feelings with you that I'd never felt before, and I didn't know how to handle it.'

He drew her closer against him, burying his face in her hair. 'All the time I was in the States I've been going frantic—I must have picked up the phone to call you a hundred times, to apologise for being such a crass idiot, to beg you to give me another chance. But I didn't know what to say.'

She wrapped her arms around him, oblivious of her surroundings, her heart spilling over. 'That night,' she whispered. 'It wasn't... The reason I didn't want you to come home with me—it wasn't what you thought. I——'

'I know.' He placed a gentle finger across her lips. 'Sir Richard told me about it—weeks ago. He said when he first heard your name that it rang a bell—it took him a while to remember why. Why didn't you ever tell me yourself? I've told you things about me I've never told anyone else.'

Her cheeks tinged with pink, and she lowered her eyes. 'I... don't know,' she stammered unsteadily. 'I thought... You'd been attracted to the image you had of me, and I was afraid to change it in case... you didn't like the difference.'

'Idiot,' he chided her softly, his eyes warm. 'It was when I began to recognise the hurt behind that proud front you put on that I began to realise that I was falling in love with you.'

'I... I didn't know,' she whispered, gazing up at him. 'I was so much in love with you, but I was afraid to tell you. I thought... if you knew, you'd run a mile, so I kept pretending...' Something he had said a few moments earlier struck her mind with the force of a ten-ton truck. 'Did you say you wanted to marry me?' she queried in astonishment.

'Yes.' He smiled down into her misted eyes. 'Will you?'

'Oh, yes...!' she breathed, no longer hiding the love in her heart. 'Oh, yes, please.'

He bent his head to claim her mouth in a kiss of the sweetest tenderness, and she responded totally, not caring who might be watching. She had dreamed of this so many times, never believing it could become real; but the feeling of his strong arms around her forced her to the conclusion that if this was an illusion it was a remarkably solid one...

The sound of footsteps, and her mother's startled voice, cut through the spell. 'Alysha? Good heavens—what on earth...?'

'Oh...!' Her cheeks flamed scarlet as she pulled back out of Ross's arms. 'Er... Mummie, this is Ross Elliot—you remember, I told you about him. He... runs the advertising agency that's doing the Lozier campaign.'

To her surprise, Ross rose to the occasion magnificently. Taking the astonished Audrey's hand, he gazed into her eyes, turning on the full power of that irresistible charm. 'Ah—I can see now where Alysha gets her stunning looks from,' he declared smoothly. 'It's obvious they run in the family.'

Audrey dimpled with pleasure, instantly succumbing to his outrageous flattery. 'Oh ... Well, how very nice to meet you, Mr Elliot,' she responded graciously. 'Alysha, dear, you needn't wait for me— Gerald is taking me to lunch.' There was a glint of feminine triumph in the smile she bestowed on the distinguished-looking solicitor hovering at her side. 'I can't say what time I'll be home.'

And with that she swept regally away, disdainfully aloof from her unpleasant surroundings, shielded by her precious mink from any uncomfortable reality she preferred to ignore.

Alysha gurgled with laughter. 'Well, there's a thing! Dear old Gerald—he's had a soft spot for her for years. He was Daddy's solicitor, but he was really more of a family friend—and he's a widower.'

Ross glanced down at her, smiling. 'So?'

'So wouldn't it be funny if they got together after all these years?' she chuckled. 'They might even get married!'

He laughed. 'I think that would be a very good idea,' he remarked with heartfelt sincerity. 'Especially if she's planning to do any more driving— she could save herself a fortune in legal fees! Besides, you've looked after her for quite long enough,' he added decisively. 'It's time someone else took over. You're going to have your hands full looking after me.'

That thought was so pleasant that she couldn't resist giving him a hug, which turned to another long, lingering kiss. But as he let his hand slide down the length of her spine, drawing her intimately close, she drew back, her cheeks flaming scarlet.

'Ross!' she protested in a husky whisper. 'Stop it—this really isn't the place. People are beginning to stare...'

He conceded with a chuckle, setting her on her feet. 'All right. But the register office is in the next building to this one. We're going over there right now to sort out a special licence. And then you can ring Alain and ask him to send that dress over on the next plane. I intend to make this relationship legal and binding before you can change your mind.'

'Oh, I won't change my mind,' she promised, laying her head against his shoulder. 'You can have all the commitment in the world. That's all I ever wanted—now and for ever.'

Return this coupon and we'll send you 4 Mills & Boon romances and a mystery gift absolutely FREE! We'll even pay the postage and packing for you.

We're making you this offer to introduce you to the benefits of Reader Service: FREE home delivery of brand-new Mills & Boon romances, at least a month before they are available in the shops, FREE gifts and a monthly Newsletter packed with information.

Accepting these FREE books and gift places you under no obligation to buy, you may cancel at any time, even after receiving just your free shipment. Simply complete the coupon below and send it to:

HARLEQUIN MILLS & BOON, FREEPOST, PO BOX 70, CROYDON, CR9 9EL.

No stamp needed

Yes, please send me 4 free Mills & Boon romances and a mystery gift. I understand that unless you hear from me, I will receive 6 superb new titles every month for just £1.99* each postage and packing free. I am under no obligation to purchase any books and I may cancel or suspend my subscription at any time, but the free books and gifts will be mine to keep in any case. (I am over 18 years of age)

1EP5R

Ms/Mrs/Miss/Mr _____

Address _____

_____

_____ Postcode _____

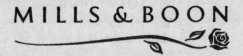

MILLS & BOON

Next Month's Romances

Each month you can choose from a wide variety of romance with Mills & Boon. Below are the new titles to look out for next month.

DEADLY RIVALS	Charlotte Lamb
TREACHEROUS LONGINGS	Anne Mather
THE TRUSTING GAME	Penny Jordan
WHEN ENEMIES MARRY...	Lindsay Armstrong
WANTED: WIFE AND MOTHER	Barbara McMahon
MASTER OF SEDUCTION	Sarah Holland
SAVAGE SEDUCTION	Sharon Kendrick
COME BACK FOREVER	Stephanie Howard
A FAMILY CLOSENESS	Emma Richmond
DANGEROUS NIGHTS	Rosalie Ash
HOUSE OF DREAMS	Leigh Michaels
DESERT MOON	Jennifer Taylor
PROGRESS OF PASSION	Alison Kelly
BITTERSWEET DECEPTION	Liz Fielding
UNTAMED MELODY	Quinn Wilder
RELUCTANT CHARADE	Margaret Callaghan